# Hallowed Destiny

## Forged by Darkness

*A novella in the Chattanooga Supernaturals series,*
*part of the Kirsten O'Shea Universe*

*Candace Blevins*

eXcessica publishing

**Ghost** © October 2016 by Candace Blevins

Excessica LLC
P.O. Box 127
Alpena, MI 49707

To order additional copies of this book, contact:
books@excessica.com
www.excessica.com

Cover design © 2016 Syneca Featherstone
First Edition October 2016

It's been a year since Destiny was abducted by sick demon worshipers who intended to use her as a human sacrifice. They'd already carved evil-looking symbols all over her body when she somehow managed to escape.

Tonight is Halloween — the one-year anniversary of her abduction — and she's determined to return to the woods where she nearly lost her life. She doesn't expect to see a white lion waiting for her. Aren't black cats supposed to be bad luck on Halloween? Perhaps a white lion will be the opposite of evil. Or, maybe she's finally lost her mind, because lions are *not* indigenous to Tennessee and Georgia.

Candace loves hearing from readers! You can find her online at:

- Website – candaceblevins.com
- Facebook - facebook.com/candacesblevins
- Facebook group – Candace's Kinksters - facebook.com/groups/CandacesKinksters
- Twitter - @CandaceBlevins
- Goodreads - goodreads.com/CandaceBlevins

Stay up to date on Candace's newest releases and get exclusive excerpts by joining her mailing list - http://eepurl.com/W_Cij

# Chapter One

*Destiny*

I parked at a diner just outside the Chickamauga Battlefield and pulled my bicycle out of the back of my SUV. I made sure my phone was in one pocket, pepper spray in another, and felt my exercise bra to be sure my dad's two-hundred-dollar flashlight was still secure. I hadn't told him I was borrowing it because I didn't want to answer all the questions about why I needed it. As far as my family was concerned, I was spending the night with a friend and staying in where it was safe.

A year ago tonight — Halloween — I'd been abducted by sick demon worshipers, and would've been killed by them as a human sacrifice had I not found a way to escape. They carved symbols into the flesh of my chest, stomach, thighs, feet, and hands. I'd forever have to wear bangs to hide the scars on my forehead.

On my eighteenth birthday two weeks ago, I'd had the first part of an extensive tattoo started on my chest. I planned to cover the horrible, *evil* scars with something beautiful, but it'd take a while.

Dread pooled in my stomach as I pedaled toward the spot I'd been staked to the ground. They'd stripped me naked and spread me out so it was impossible to hide any part of myself from them. They'd apparently wanted a virgin to kill in offering to whatever sick deity they worship.

To keep it from happening again, I'd planned to have sex with the first person who came along afterwards, but it hadn't worked out. The asshole I'd been dating — the one who'd claimed to be a *good Christian boy* — broke up with me two days later because he was afraid the marks on my skin made me evil.

Much to my parents' chagrin, I'd turned my back on the church and started dating the star quarterback at the local high school — with every intention of giving myself to him at the first opportunity, though they weren't aware of that last part. He lived two doors down so it hadn't been difficult to sneak and see him when I told them I was going for a bike ride.

Unfortunately, I'd freaked and started crying when he got my panties off, and he'd told me I was too high maintenance.

So a year later I was still a damned virgin, and may end up staying that way. Those *fuckers* had messed me up in the head, and when the quarterback had undressed me, my only thoughts in were how I'd felt when my kidnappers had stripped me and staked me spread-eagled on the ground.

My pastor's wife told me I needed to find a way to put this behind me — to close the door on it and look forward. I wasn't sure how to do that but figured going back to the scene of the crime on Halloween night was a good start. I'd researched the area on Google Earth and found what I hoped was the best spot to ride my bike into the woods. I looked all around to be sure no cars were near, and flicked my bike's headlight off as I veered into the pitch dark of the forest.

I stopped a few yards in because I couldn't see *anything*, and I planted my feet on either side of my bike and waited for my eyes to adjust to the dark. My heart raced and my pulse thundered in my ears, but I assured myself no one else could hear it.

Several long minutes later, I thought I might be able to pick out the trees, but not well enough to walk, much less ride. I propped my bike on a tree with a sigh, and turned the flashlight to the lowest setting. I hadn't planned to use it this close to the road, but it didn't look like I had a choice.

Each step forward took every bit of willpower I possessed. I wanted to turn and run back to the road, but I just *knew* I'd never move past this unless I could face my fears. If I could walk into the woods on Halloween and stand in the spot I'd fought my abductors, perhaps I'd be brave enough to have sex with someone and finally lose my pesky virginity.

I counted fifty steps before I turned the flashlight a little brighter, and I pulled my phone from my pocket and re-engaged the directions to the GPS coordinates I'd chosen. I hoped the location I'd found on the map would get me close enough so I'd be able to find *the spot* once I was nearby.

I had crazy dreams about that night. It often felt more like I'd been rescued, but I also kind of vaguely remembered getting an arm free and grabbing the knife from one of the men, and then going to town on my kidnappers as I cut myself free. But then there was the dream where a woman levitated me up to sit on a tree branch while monsters fought monsters. Were there good monsters? Some of them looked half-human and half-animal, truly grotesque... and yet in my dreams they fought the evil men who'd abducted me.

I had less than a quarter mile to walk, but it felt like I crept miles in the dark — carefully placing each foot and listening for sounds of anything larger than a possum while my own pulse thundered in my ears.

When I finally arrived at the GPS spot, I turned my dad's flashlight to full strength — all twenty-eight hundred lumens.

And was shocked to see a white lion sitting fifty yards away.

I couldn't move. Couldn't breathe. My feet were cemented to the ground as the lion looked down and away as the too-bright light must've hurt his eyes.

Two seconds later he turned and gracefully leapt through the air, and within seconds he'd run off to the side and out of the beam. I turned the light in every direction but couldn't find him again. Had I hallucinated him? Lions are *not* indigenous to Tennessee. Or Georgia. Crap, I was just over the line in Georgia. Didn't matter. There shouldn't be a lion.

# Chapter Two

*Zeke*

I shifted to human and dressed as quickly as possible. What the fuck was Destiny doing here? And what the hell kind of flashlight had she been using? She'd have never seen me with a regular flashlight, but I was in deep shit for letting her see my lion. Destiny was in deeper shit, though, unless I could convince her she'd seen something else.

I laced my boots, stood, and ran my hand through my hair. I traced my fingers through the scraggly beard I always have when I came back from lion, and sighed as I followed my nose back to her.

Her already racing heart began to beat even faster as I walked towards her, and she cautiously asked, "Who's there?"

I was ready for the bright light this time when it swung my direction, plus I could throw an arm over my eyes in this form.

I smelled her relief a half-second before she asked, "Zeke? What are you doing here?"

"Making sure the group those assholes are part of doesn't bring someone else to the same place tonight. Why are you here?"

She sighed as she turned her flashlight down and pointed it to the left enough so the beam no longer hit me directly. "I needed to come back. I don't know why, and I can't explain it."

"You need to face your fears, but you shouldn't have come alone." I should get bonus points for not adding *you crazy-assed human* to the end of my sentence.

She gave a nervous laugh. "I know this sounds crazy, but have you seen... *no*. It's stupid."

I walked with her as she headed toward the hill where we'd found her staked out on the ground. "How'd you know where to find the exact spot?"

"I remembered how far we were from the creek and about how long it took to come out in the field near the tower. I wasn't sure I could find the *exact* spot, but I remember that tree."

I followed her flashlight's beam as she spotlit the limb Kirsten had levitated them to. She wasn't supposed to remember anything supernatural, and yet she remembered the branch.

I thought I was in the clear with her seeing my lion. I thought she'd convinced herself she'd imagined it, and perhaps I was right. However, I hadn't expected her to look for signs of the lion, and my heart fell into my stomach as her flashlight landed on a tuft of my nearly-white fur. When I'd turned and leapt, some of my mane had gotten caught on a branch.

*Fuck.*

"I didn't imagine him."

With a sigh, I sat on the ground and tried to look relaxed as I said, "That lion will never hurt you. Sit with me so I can explain?"

She shook her head, and I straightened my legs in front of me and leaned back on my elbows. "I know you remember stuff that doesn't make sense. I can't explain any of it to you, but I can tell you about the lion. I need you to sit with me, though. Would I be doing this if I thought there was any threat at all? *Fuck*, Destiny — I took care of you and didn't leave your side for days while you were in the hospital. Even after we'd contacted your family and got them down there, I stuck around to be sure you were safe. I'm not going to let a lion eat you now."

Finally, she sat beside me, and I sat up and said, "I'm the lion, Teeny."

"You can't be, and don't call me Teeny!"

She'd looked thirteen or fourteen when I first saw her, and now at eighteen she could still easily pass as a young teen. She says she's five feet tall, but if asked she'll admit she rounds up from four feet, eleven and a quarter inches. I'm six foot five inches tall and built like a football player. In fact, I'd played football until I was bitten by a lion at fifteen.

The Amakhosi wouldn't be pleased I'd done this without consulting him, but I hoped he'd understand. I took a deep breath, found my center, and trusted the lion would be on board with showing himself in the least traumatic way I could think of.

My left hand was in the dark since she sat to my right, so I *changed* it into a lion's paw. When the transformation was complete, I pulled it around so she could see. "It's just my paw. I don't want to do a complete *change* and scare you. Shine the light on it and look. You can touch it if you want — just keep your hands on the top. My claws are sheathed but we want to make sure I don't scratch you."

Her heart sped, then slowed. Her scent went from shocked and afraid to something close to relief. "I've dreamed of monsters fighting monsters. Why do I dream it, but I can't remember?"

"Why are you relieved?"

"How do you know I'm relieved? The werewolves in the books I've been reading can smell fear. Can you smell relief?"

"Yeah, Teeny. I can smell all your emotions."

"That's how you took such good care of me while I was in the hospital?" She shook her head and looked off into the dark forest. "You knew when I was afraid or when I hurt, even if I didn't tell anyone."

"How are your parents?" They'd been terrified of their daughter at first, afraid she'd been turned evil. I honestly think they'd have refused to let her come home if the bastards had gone so far as raping her. They'd treated her

14

more like a stranger than a daughter until the doctor confirmed she was still a virgin.

"They threatened to kick me out when I refused to go to church, but our pastor actually took my side and told them to give me time. We reached a compromise, and I have dinner with his family once a month, and spend an hour or two talking to his wife after we eat." She shrugged. "They don't know about my tattoo yet." She touched her chest. "When it's finished, it'll hide the scars. I always wear high neck shirts so no one can see my scars, it's just covering the tattoo now. I probably won't show them until I can afford to move out."

For such a little thing, she was so fucking strong. I wanted to see the tattoo, wanted to know what she'd designed, but it felt too personal, so I asked, "You're working?"

"I'm doing okay teaching private lessons for piano, guitar, and violin. I'm at UTC this year — going for a business major, with a minor in music."

She'd been homeschooled and had graduated early, but I was surprised her parents were letting her go to a non-religious college. I decided not to bring it up, though. "How are you handling regular classes? You've never had to learn that way, have you?"

"It's okay. I was terrified at first, but I've learned it's more annoying than difficult. Your hand's back to normal."

"My hand's back to *human*. It's normal for me to be a lion sometimes."

"So, you're a werelion?"

I sighed. The night had gotten complicated, and it had the potential to go all wrong. "We usually say lion shifter, but werelion isn't wrong. Humans can't know about us, but I had no idea you'd have a flashlight brighter than the fucking sun. Since you know, there's a procedure we have to follow to make it... well, legal, I guess. Did you drive?"

"My car's outside the park at a fast food restaurant, and I left my bike just inside the woods."

I pulled my phone out of my jeans and texted the Drake Security control room to let them know I needed someone to replace me the rest of the night, and I'd need a private audience with the Amakhosi — preferably well before morning.

* * * *

I watched as His Majesty prepared Destiny's wine with a little of his blood in it. Her blood was already in a small glass of water, and we'd traumatized her all over again when we had to get it. The Celrau had decorated themselves with her blood, and there'd been no way to get some of hers into the glass without reminding her of what they'd done.

She was a trooper though. It helped that she remembered His Majesty was one of the people who arrived to rescue her last year. Of course, her memory is of escaping and calling for help, and we were part of the SWAT team that responded. Never mind none of us were wearing uniforms. Hell, never mind most of us weren't entirely human as we fought. Abbott had altered her memories, but I was wondering if the vampire had made a mistake when he wiped the parts she wasn't supposed to remember.

I hadn't seen Destiny in over ten months, and yet I still felt this fierce need to protect her. She was seventeen back then — to my twenty-five — so pulling away from her was my only option. A seventeen year old looking to lose her virginity is like a ticking time bomb under the best of circumstances, and with my protective streak and crazy attraction to her, it hadn't been the best of circumstances.

His Majesty walked her through the binding ceremony, making it so she can't tell any supernatural secrets. He was gentle and patient, answering her questions, soothing her fears, but firm about making sure it was done correctly. When the binding was complete and he'd tested it, he glanced at me before telling her, "Zeke tells me you've had dreams you can't explain. He thinks they're what made you go back into the woods tonight. I'd like you to tell *me* why you went."

She looked at me and I assured her, "You're safe in this room. We want to be sure you stay safe outside of this room as well, and if we understand what precipitated the risky behavior, perhaps we can help keep it from happening again. You're an adult — you get to make your own decisions, but we'd like to help you make smarter decisions if we can."

"I've dreamed of a woman levitating me to a tree branch, way up in the air, and I saw the branch tonight. I *recognized* it." She looked from me to His Majesty. "I've dreamed of half-men and half-animals fighting the men who took me, and then it turns out Zeke can turn part-lion. I've dreamed of the men who abducted me doing strange things, *impossible* things. I've also dreamed them with long fangs and translucent skin." She stood and took three steps to a window, her back to us as she looked out. "I told myself I went back because I needed to face my fears. I think part of the reason was so I could try to sort through the memories versus the dreams, because the dreams feel more real than the memories."

His Majesty's gaze met mine, and I held it long enough I hoped he saw I wanted her to know the truth. I didn't hold it long before I lowered my gaze though. Some people respect the Amakhosi because he'll make them hurt if they don't, but I respect him because he found me when no one was looking for me. He'd killed the asshole who'd raped and bitten me, and then he'd helped me learn control. Little did I know that when I'd prayed for *someone* to help me, there was a lion out there who'd hear.

"Did I see the tree branch while I was staked to the ground, and my imagination put it into my dreams later? Or am I going crazy?" Destiny's back was still to us, and I got the feeling she was terrified of the answer but also scared of never knowing the truth.

"Someone altered your memories, Destiny," Nathan told her, and I breathed in relief. "You couldn't know about werelions, so we had someone make you forget. I'm hesitant to offer to have them restored because I know you've refused therapy." He sighed, and I could tell he was trying not to sound aggravated as he gently asked, "Can you please come sit down, or at least turn around? I don't like speaking to the back of your head."

She shook her head and kept her back to us, and I walked to her, stepped in front of her, and pulled her into my arms. That was all it took to get the waterworks started. I had no idea what to say or do, so I held her as she cried.

Several minutes into it, she managed to say, "I always *knew* there was more! I wasn't crazy! I'm *not* crazy!"

I rubbed her back and looked at His Majesty for help, but he stretched his legs out in front of the chair and looked as if he was getting comfortable. I'd brought her to my house, and His Majesty had been waiting in the driveway when we arrived.

Several long minutes later I bent so I could pick her up like an infant, and I carried her to the sofa. She molded into my arms and let me, and settled into my lap when I sat. I held her head to my shoulder, supporting it more than holding, and had to fight the urge to kiss the top of her head.

"I'm glad you're comfortable with Zeke," Nathan said. I've seen the Amakhosi's soft side, but it's been a while and my heart warmed at the tenderness in his voice. "I'm friends with a therapist, and I think you'll like her. She knows about supernaturals and she was present when we rescued you. You can talk to her about anything, but she won't answer any questions — she'll just help you work through whatever's in your head. If you see her eight times, I'll talk to her about the pros and cons of having the person who altered your memories put them back."

She started to argue, but I interrupted. "He's right, Teeny. If he won't cover the costs of therapy then I will. I couldn't do much of anything when you were still a minor, but you're an adult now, and if your parents kick you out of the house then you can crash here until you can afford a place." *Fuck*, I was out of my ever-loving mind, but I couldn't stomach the thought of her refusing therapy because she was afraid of being kicked out of her parents' house.

His Majesty lifted an eyebrow at my offer, but merely said, "I'll get the therapist's information to Zeke so you can call and make an appointment. She's on my payroll and I'll cover the eight visits." He stood and looked at me. "Step outside with me a moment."

I followed him to my front porch, and he asked, "Are you sure about this?"

"No, but she's an adult now." I shook my head. "I wish I could've been there over the last year, but I knew it wasn't possible. I did all I could for her and things are different now. She's legally an adult, she's in college, and she's beginning to make plans to move out of her parents' house. I'm going to do what I can to help her."

He pulled me into a hug and I relaxed in his arms. The Amakhosi is the king of all lions on the planet. He's the leader of the local pride as well, but he's still the man who rescued me and looked out for me. He's like my second father.

"If I haven't told you lately, I'm proud of the man you've grown into. I'm leaving her in your care, but I'll expect you to let me know if you need help with anything." He released me from the hug and took a step back. "Under normal circumstances you'd have felt my fist or my whip for showing her a partial *change* without my permission, but I agree it was the right decision. Don't let it make you cocky if you find yourself in the same situation again though."

"I understand, Your Majesty."

"I'm not joking about being kept in the loop. I want regular updates, and I'll be pissed if I find out you needed help and didn't let me know."

"I need to get her car here. It's in Fort O." I wasn't sure what his silence meant, so I explained. "The rules say once I've shown her what I am, she has to stay in my presence until she's bound. I couldn't let her follow me."

"I know. I was considering logistics. Why don't I drive the two of you to it now, and then you can drive her back here in it."

# Chapter Three

*Destiny*

I awakened the next morning in a strange room, and it took a few seconds for the events of the night before to flood my brain.

*I was in Zeke's guest bedroom, wearing one of his shirts as pajamas.*

My face flamed hot again at the thoughts of being in any state of undress in his *house*. In his *bed*. Even if it isn't the bed he sleeps in, he still owns it.

I looked at the clock in a panic and relaxed back into the sheets when I saw it wasn't quite eight o'clock yet. My first class on Tuesday and Thursday isn't until ten, so I wasn't late. He'd told me last night he had to be in court at nine, so I figured he was up already. I keep extra clothes in my car, and I'd showered before getting into bed so now

I only had to slide into my jeans, t-shirt, and hoodie. My parents hate the new way I dress, but it feels right to me.

*If blue jeans are a sin then I'm tired of listening to God.* My mom had slapped me across the face for saying it, but it's ten months later and I still feel the same.

I brushed my teeth, pulled my hair into a ponytail, and went to Zeke's living room, but didn't see him. I heard something behind me and I turned as he stepped into the room.

"I was in my office looking over my notes before I walk into court. I'll be leaving in about ten minutes so I'm glad you're up. How'd you sleep?"

"Fine, thanks again for letting me stay. I can grab my stuff and leave when you do."

"Nonsense. You have over an hour until your first class. There's eggs and bacon in the fridge — you're welcome to fix whatever you find, just please lock the door on your way out and text me that you've left. I can set my alarm remotely."

Zeke is gorgeous in jeans and a t-shirt, but he's *beautiful* in a suit. He hadn't put his jacket on yet, but the pants were a dark charcoal, his shirt was a crisp white, and his black tie had little diagonal charcoal stripes.

"You trust me here when you aren't?"

"I told you last night — if you get kicked out of your parents' house for going to therapy, you're more than welcome to stay here until you can figure out a place of your own. I emailed you the therapist's name this morning already. You need to call her office and set a time for your

Candace Blevins

first appointment. If you don't have plans for tomorrow evening, I'd like to have dinner with you."

"I have a private lesson from five until six, and they live in Ooltewah."

"I can pick you up at six-thirty at your house, or you can meet me at The Boathouse at seven. Up to you."

"I'll meet you there."

"Give me a hug before I go?"

Zeke's arms have represented safety to me from the beginning. I was in shock when Nathan had first handed me over to him, and Zeke held me without caring how bloody I was — and didn't let go of me until the medical people insisted. He didn't leave my side for days, other than to go to the bathroom, and even then he left the door cracked and talked to me. He had people bring him food several times a day so he could stay with me in my hospital room. I was terrified, and somehow I just *knew* no one would hurt me with him around to protect me.

My dad hadn't wanted Zeke anywhere near me, but he'd had credentials saying he was a professional bodyguard and told them he'd been assigned to watch me while I was in the hospital. He pointed out my dad couldn't legally carry in the hospital, but Zeke had permission from the administration and could make sure I wasn't abducted again.

"Are you really a bodyguard?" I asked now. "You're an attorney — most people aren't both."

"I'm trained as a bodyguard and worked my way through college as one. I keep my credentials up, though I only do enough work these days to stay officially active."

He stepped to a closet near the front door, pulled his suit jacket out, and slid his arms into it. My face and lower body grew warm as I wondered how gentle he'd be if *he* was the one who took my virginity.

He ran his fingers through his hair and down his clean-shaven face, and at the same moment I realized he'd cut his hair and shaved, I also realized he could probably smell my physical attraction for him.

I put my hands over my face in embarrassment, and he chuckled. "In the spirit of fairness, if you could scent my reactions you'd know I'd love to have you in my bed as well." He stepped to me and gently pulled my hands away from my face. I practically fell into his clear blue eyes as he said, "I don't know if it's appropriate, but it isn't illegal anymore, so that's something. I'll see you tomorrow at The Boathouse."

I nodded, he kissed my forehead, and then he was gone.

# Chapter Four

*Zeke*

The next evening, His Majesty texted me to let me know Destiny had seen the therapist at three o'clock. She'd had a cancellation, and Destiny's final class had ended at ten minutes before three, just a few blocks away. His Majesty also sent me Destiny's class schedule, and what he could easily learn of her private tutoring calendar — as well as the fact she charged from forty-five to sixty dollars an hour, depending on the instrument and type of instruction needed.

I've seen her playing on YouTube videos, but I've yet to hear her play in person. I needed to rectify that immediately.

She pulled into the restaurant parking lot, and I walked to her SUV to greet her.

"How was your day?" I asked.

"Busy, but I got a lot accomplished. How'd your court case go yesterday?"

"Not guilty, thank goodness. Nathan let me know you saw the therapist — do you think you'll want to go back?"

"I… *maybe*." She shrugged and looked toward the Tennessee River a second before focusing on where she was walking once again. "I liked her and she made me feel comfortable. I was cross about having to go — it felt a little like coercion, ya know? *You have to do this thing you don't want to do, or we won't give you your memories back.*"

"Felt? So you don't feel that way anymore?"

"She explained why he's being cautious and I understand a little better now. It still feels like someone with power making the rules just because he can, but I also get that he doesn't want to do more harm than good, and he needs Kirsten to tell him whether I can handle getting it all at once, or whether I should get a little at a time, or whether I'm a weak little baby who isn't strong enough to be told the truth."

"I doubt that's the way she worded it, but yeah, he wants to be sure he doesn't cause more pain than necessary. If there's anything I can do to help, you only need to let me know."

"Thanks. Why are you being so good to me? Is Nathan paying you again?"

"Nathan didn't pay me before, and he certainly isn't now."

She stopped dead and stared at me, clearly confused.

I sighed, pulled her out of the middle of the parking lot, stopped between some cars, and touched her chin. "I was paid to babysit the site on Halloween night this year, and I was paid to help with the rescue party last year, but that's it. It worked out I could stay with you in the hospital, but if you'd stayed a day longer I'd have had to bring someone else in to watch you so I could work. Once you were home, your parents wouldn't let us guard you anymore, but by that point I felt certain you were safe from other supernatural elements who might want you for their purposes."

"I liked having you around, but I thought you were only there because it was your job."

"I was there because you needed me, and because something inside me..." I trailed off as I remembered I could be honest with her now. "And because my lion is fiercely protective of you. He's pissed someone hurt you, and he wants to make sure you're never hurt again. Nathan tasked me with getting you to the hospital and handing you over to family. You were safe, but you were scared, so I stayed." Abbott had adjusted her aura when he'd rearranged her memories. She no longer gave off the vibe of a virgin, and if the marks and symbols made on her were meant to send out signals, his manipulations would keep them from doing so.

She looked at the restaurant and back to me. "We can't talk about this stuff here, can we? Should we get food and take it somewhere?"

I shook my head. "We'll eat here and have normal conversation, and if you want to follow me back to my place afterwards, we can talk about whatever else you want to discuss."

She nodded, and I took her hand and walked her inside.

I started our dinner conversation by asking about her six siblings, and before long I had her telling me about her classes at UTC and the friends she's made.

When that conversation seemed to be coming to an end, I asked, "You said you have dinner with your pastor and his wife once a month?"

She nodded. "He says it's normal for people to have a crisis of faith after a trauma. I expected to hate having bible study with his wife after dinner, but she's made it relevant to my life and hasn't preached to me so much as asked me what I get out of scripture. Once, she just opened the Bible at random and said we'd let God speak to us, and it was kind of bizarre because it all fit." She shook her head. "I don't think my parents' church is right about a lot of their beliefs. Other churches read the same Bible and believe different things, so I'm not alone in that. I don't know what the answer is, but I'm beginning to think as long as I follow the Ten Commandments and what I just *know* to be right and wrong — I dunno, but I think that may be the best I can do."

"Sounds pretty healthy to me. Have you gone to any college parties at all?"

"Yeah, and I drank a little at one, then a lot at the next, and decided drinking isn't all it's cracked up to be."

I laughed. "I'd love to see you tipsy, but even more, I want to hear you play. Do you have your violin with you? I don't have a piano."

She shook her head. "I don't, but if you want to stop by the Fine Arts building with me, we can use one of the piano practice rooms." She wrinkled her brow. "But why do you want to hear me play?"

"Your music seems to be a big part of who you are, and I'm hoping you'll let me get to know you better."

* * * *

I live in one of the historic houses in the Fortwood District, and only about a block and a half away from the Fine Arts building. My house was in bad shape when I bought it, and I liked the location more than the old house part because I'm less than five minutes from work even in heavy traffic. I've done a lot of work to try to keep it from just being a drafty old house with beautiful architectural details. My master suite is made up of three bedrooms — I turned one into a large bathroom, and another into a huge closet.

Destiny directed me to park at the back of the Fine Arts building and used her student ID card to open the tiny little practice cubicle. It was really only big enough for one person, but she had me sit beside her on the bench.

My lion didn't like the little soundproof, claustrophobic room — we couldn't smell or hear anyone in the hallway — but I placated him with the reminder she'd needed the card to open the door.

"What do you want me to play?"

"Whatever brings you joy."

"Of all the times I've asked that question, no one's ever given me that answer."

She put her fingers to the keys and my heart sang as beautiful music filled the tiny room.

I recognized the tune but had no idea what it was. I was pretty sure it was classical, but beyond that I was clueless. It didn't matter though, because every cell in my body seemed to resonate with the tune, the beat, the vibrations. It was as if my soul was set free in the tiny room.

When the last notes finally faded, I was silent a good ten seconds before I could find my voice to speak.

"I don't know what to say, other than you made my heart happy with your music. I recognized it, or rather, I've heard it before so it was familiar, but I have no idea what it was."

"It's a Bach piece — *Jesu, Joy of Man's Desiring.* Here, I'll play something you're more familiar with."

I smiled as I heard the first notes to *Bohemian Rhapsody.* My lion was fascinated as her fingers seemed to stroke some keys and caress others. What would those hands feel like on my cock?

And then her hands began an odd combination of pounding and stroking, and I was mesmerized. Such fucking talent.

But the music! I had goosebumps. I felt my damned nipples hardening. She pulled emotions out of me with a seventies song.

As the final notes died away, I pulled her to me, speechless. When I finally managed words, I could only say, "You're amazing."

If I hadn't already loved her, this would've been the moment I realized I was head-over-heels for her. Talent is nice, but you have to cultivate it and work at it to turn it into true skill. This tiny little human had the gumption and the perseverance to hone her talents. She'd been tortured by Celrau and bore their foul scars, and she could *still* make beautiful music.

I wanted her in my life, but I was going to have to be careful not to fuck it up.

# Chapter Five

*Destiny*

I had so many questions I wasn't sure where to start.

"A few ground rules," he told me as he used an electronic keypad to open his front door. "I can tell you almost anything about me, but I can't tell you about other people."

"I've dreamt of wolves, too. Or, half-wolves, I think." I shook my head. "I'm pretty sure the therapist is the woman who levitated me up to the tree branch, too."

"Did you ask her about it?"

I shook my head. "I figured maybe I shouldn't let the therapist know just how crazy I might be."

Zeke sat on a sofa and leaned forward with his face in his hands a few seconds before he sat back and met my gaze.

"I met Nathan when he rescued me. I was sixteen." He looked away a few seconds before looking back at me. "I was kidnapped and raped at fifteen, and the fuckwad turned into a lion and bit me after the fourth or fifth time he raped me. I wasn't born a lion, I was turned." He looked away, his eyes not focused on anything in the room. "He had me for months before Nathan found me. No one was looking for me, but he happened to travel close enough he could feel my distress. A regular lion can't do that, but Nathan's pretty powerful and I'm lucky he came close enough to feel something wrong and check it out."

I didn't know what to say, so I kneeled on the sofa beside his legs, facing him, and leaned in to hug him.

"I'm okay now, Teeny. Nathan made sure of it, and now I want to make sure you're okay. Nathan's in charge, but he's given me leave to take care of you as long as I report in to him."

"Who is he to you?"

"You said you'd been reading about werewolves, so you understand the concept of the Alpha Wolf, right?"

I nodded and he said, "Think of him as the leader of our Pride."

"So you have to do what he says?"

"I do, but I love and respect him, and I'd follow his orders even if I didn't have to."

"You love him? Are you..." How do you ask if someone's gay without insulting them?

Thankfully, he chuckled. "No, I like women, and my lion and I both *really* like you. I love Nathan like a father, or a patriarch. He saved my life and has made sure I lived it to my fullest potential ever since."

"You're a criminal attorney? Do you defend the bad guys?"

He smiled. "I can smell a lie. When I decide whether to take a case or not, I know if they're guilty. Sometimes I take their case even if they're guilty, but I base it on my own personal morals. If it was a mostly victimless crime, I'll do my best to get them off or work out a fair plea-bargain. If they killed someone's kid and deserve prison, or worse? No way will I take the case."

I took a breath and asked what I most wanted to know. "You said you wanted me in your bed?"

His clear blue eyes softened and he gave me a sad smile as he cupped my face in his huge hands. "I do, but even more, I want to be sure you're okay. It was years after I was raped before I could be intimate with anyone, and I was the one doing the fu…" He stopped himself and said it a different way. "I wasn't the one being entered, and I *still* couldn't be intimate. You weren't raped, but you were violated. How have you handled intimacy with other men?"

My eyes filled with tears, and he pulled me onto his lap and tucked my head against his chest as his arms surrounded me. I'd always known I was safe in his arms, and now I was even more certain of it.

When I could trust my voice, I told him, "You're the only person who's been able to hold me like this without me freaking out a little."

"If you see me as safe, no way can I do anything to risk that."

"I tried to have sex. The guy was an asshole, but he was nice to me once I let him know I was interested in him, and he kissed good, and I figured I just needed to get rid of my virginity so no one else would try to sacrifice me." I took a breath to finish the story, but my tears came and I couldn't speak. Zeke didn't tell me not to cry, he didn't assure me everything was okay, he just held me as I sobbed in his arms.

Several minutes passed before I had enough control of my voice to continue. "I managed to keep from freaking out until he took my underwear off, and then I lost it. I remember feeling so vulnerable, and exposed, and *helpless*, and it all came back. My parents tried to marry me off at first, saying I needed a husband to properly care for me, but we had a few huge fights about it and they finally agreed to let me go to a college of my choosing if I could figure out a way to pay for it myself."

"I'm proud of you. It can't have been easy to stand up to your parents. I know they love you, but they have some pretty strong and inflexible beliefs."

"Where are your parents?"

He shook his head and looked away. "They were killed by the man who abducted me. He tossed their car off a cliff with them in it, and set fire to it at the bottom of the ravine. He put another kid in the backseat, where I'd have been, so it was assumed the three of us died. No one knew to look for me. He meant to keep me as his."

"What happened to him?"

"Nathan offered to let me kill him, but I couldn't. He let me watch him die, though." He shrugged, his blue eyes dark. "There've been times I've wished he'd died at my hand, and other times I'm glad it wasn't me who did it. He's dead, and that's the important part."

Murder's wrong, but I couldn't find fault with him being happy the man who'd killed his parents and repeatedly raped him was dead. My memories are of killing my abductors in self-defense, though my dreams are of the half-monsters killing them. Either way, I'm glad they're dead.

Zeke's lips touched the top of my head, and I smiled at how close I felt to him. His voice rumbled through his chest as he continued. "My sister's a lot older than me, and she was overseas when everything happened. She's back now, and we're close. She thought she'd lost us all, so having me back was like getting her brother back from the dead."

"The first night, in the hospital, you never left my side. You even knew when everything got to be too much, and you asked the nurses and police people to give me ten minutes alone, and worked it so they came back one at a time to get what they needed from me. You knew to do that because you lived through something like it?"

"My situation was different, but I knew they freaked you the fuck out. They were trying to be gentle, but it was too much, too fast."

"I woke up once and you were in the hospital bed with me, holding me." We'd never talked about it. Once I was awake and okay, he'd gotten back in the chair.

"You were having a nightmare, so I held you and kept telling you I had you, and you were safe, until it went away." He shrugged again. "If you wake someone from a nightmare, they remember it and it seeps into real life. If you can make it go away, they usually won't remember it."

"I looked you up. You became an attorney three years ago, when I think you'd have just been twenty-three?"

"Yeah. I couldn't handle going back to high school — because my lion wasn't totally under control yet, and because of what had been done to me. Nathan helped me get my GED at sixteen, and I started UTC in the fall. My lion was under enough control by then. You don't really have to make friends to survive college, and I wasn't ready to get close to anyone yet." He shrugged. "I passed the bar at twenty-two, and took my first solo case at twenty-three."

"And you're twenty-six now?"

"Eight years older than you, but my lion doesn't seem to think it matters."

"But you do?"

He nodded. "I took care of you during what I'm assuming is the most traumatic time of your life. I'm not sure if it's okay — morally and ethically — to take it farther. I care about you, but I need to be sure I'm not taking advantage of you."

"If you can get rid of my pesky virginity, it might be me who's taking advantage of you."

He sighed and held me tighter. "You shouldn't say that, Teeny."

Maybe it wasn't fair, but I closed my eyes and imagined myself kissing him, imagined his hand in my panties, imagined what his penis might look like. I'd watched porn and I'd seen pictures, but I hadn't seen one in real life.

He held me tighter and groaned. "*Damn*, Teeny. This feels a little like being seduced by Mother Teresa's granddaughter. You know, if she'd had kids."

"I'm sorry. What will it take for you to be okay with..." Suddenly mortified, I felt like a small child playing in a grown up world. He didn't want me but he was trying to be nice. I pulled away from him and tried to stand, but he didn't let me go.

"This isn't rejection, Destiny. I'm not lying when I say I want you, and the lion wants you, but I also have to live with myself, so yeah, I need to be sure before we do anything."

I stopped pulling away but didn't rest my cheek on his chest again.

He sighed and asked, "How often are you seeing the therapist?"

"Twice a week."

He seemed to take a second to think it through before saying, "I'd like to take you out on a date Friday night. I'll pick you up at home, and will return you home so we don't run into us being alone here again. Give me a month, going out with me once a week, and us talking on the phone as much as we want in between. Maybe lunch a few days here and there if our schedules work out."

"You want me to have my memories back."

He shook his head. "No, I want to give you time to confront your feelings before we become intimate. I'd prefer you know what happened, but it isn't necessary before we decide to take things farther. I just need to know I gave you time with Kirsten to work through everything."

He walked me to my car and kissed my forehead before putting me in and buckling my seatbelt. "Text me when you're home safely, please?"

# Chapter Six

Five weeks later

*Destiny*

My parents hadn't been happy about me going out with Zeke, but he picked me up at six and had me home by eleven-thirty, so they didn't have much to complain about. I know my parents love me, but I also know they love God more than me. If I ever stray too far, I'll be on my own.

On this night, though, I drove to Zeke's and then Nathan picked the two of us up. I'd been told we were going to Aaron Drake's home — the owner of Drake Security — and that I'd meet the person who'd taken my memory. This unnamed person would have the final say in whether I got it back or not, and I was terrified at the prospect of meeting someone who could wander around in my head and look at my memories. Not just look at them, but *change* them if he wanted.

The curves going up Lookout Mountain were too much for me, and both werelions knew the second the nausea hit. Nathan slowed the vehicle as Zeke aimed one of the backseat vents at my face. We were in the strangest looking SUV I'd ever seen, but it was tricked out inside.

"I know ya'll can't read my mind. Or, I'm assuming you were being honest when you said you can't. Still, it's kind of weird when you know what I'm feeling before I say anything."

"If I'd known you're prone to being carsick, I'd have put you up front with Nathan," Zeke told me. "I thought you'd be better off back here by my side, so I could help keep you from being so nervous."

I looked out the front window and tried to settle my stomach with my breathing. The cool air helped, and Nathan took the curves a lot slower and easier.

"Tell me what we're walking into, please? What can I expect?"

"Aaron's wife and kids aren't home, so it'll just be the four of us, and Abbott," Nathan told me from the front seat, his eyes on me in the rearview mirror.

The mystery person finally had a name. Maybe I could ask questions now and actually get answers. "Aaron Drake is your boss — how is Abbott connected? I know he's the one who changed my memory of what happened, but how is he... who is he, to you?"

"Aaron, Abbott, and I have been friends a very long time," Nathan answered. "I'm afraid I can't tell you anything about them, but feel free to ask them any

44

questions you have. They may or may not answer, and you should choose your questions carefully because they may only give you a few answers, if they give any at all."

"I'm assuming werewolves are real, since I know werelions are. It makes sense there are lots of... species? Is that the right word?"

"If your suppositions are correct, it would make sense," Nathan answered.

"So what kind of animal can get into your memories? I keep going for things like owls or snakes, but nothing really fits."

We reached the top of the mountain and were on a straight road, finally, and I leaned back once again. Zeke touched my leg and reached for my hand. "We can't answer any of those questions, Teeny. Only Abbott can tell you what he is."

Aaron Drake lived on the brow near Point Park, and I was suitably impressed. Apparently, the security business pays well. It was well past dark outside, and the view of the city below with the lights twinkling was gorgeous.

I couldn't focus on it much, though, because I was introduced to Aaron and Abbott — complete with old-fashioned handshakes. I remembered Aaron from my rescue, but not Abbott.

I've noted before how Zeke and Nathan seem warmer than everyone else — like their resting body temperature is higher than a normal human. Aaron's hand was also warmer, but Abbott's was quite cool to the touch. My imagination immediately decided he was either a cold-blooded animal shifter like a snake or other reptile, or a vampire.

"You signed paperwork in Kirsten's office giving her permission to speak with me about how you're dealing with the events of last year," Nathan began. "I respect her opinion both as a therapist, and as someone who can help me understand how this must feel from a human perspective." He looked to Abbott and back to me. "I won't apologize for making the decisions we made. Only one in a thousand or so people realize their memories aren't right. We wanted to give you the best chance at moving forward and putting the whole situation behind you, and we thought memories of fighting your way out of a bad situation would empower you."

"There are a couple of ways I can alter memories," Abbott said. He was sitting in a fancy, armed chair, and almost looked like royalty. Actually, Aaron and Nathan looked a little like royalty too. It wasn't like they tried, but they seemed *regal*. Noble.

"I left your memories intact," Abbott told me, "but I put a wall up so you couldn't access them, and replaced the blocked portions with what we wanted you to remember. In my experience, most people do best with this approach to something traumatic. It didn't work for you, so my options at this point are to remove them entirely — to wipe that portion of your brain as if it were a hard drive on a computer — or to remove the wall and make them accessible to you."

I was still standing, and Zeke wrapped his arms around me from behind. "There are a few things you need to know ahead of time, before Abbott will consider returning your memories. Will you sit with me on the sofa, please?"

Over the next ten or fifteen minutes, I learned there are several species of vampires. Abbott is known as a Strigorii vampire. He doesn't have to kill to feed, and whether he uses his powers for good or bad is entirely up to him.

In contrast, there are Celrau vampires — the men who abducted me — who must feed once a month on the new moon, and they must kill. They need not only the blood, but also the life force of the human they drink from. Aaron explained the Celrau often work their evil in *circles*, which are basically little domes of energy designed to hold the power they're working with while keeping other forces out.

"They thrive on evil," Zeke told me, "but they didn't contaminate you with it. You weren't there as sustenance — they took your blood without biting you, and we now know they were offering you to demonkind in exchange for a deal. We knew you were being offered to a particular Demon Lord, though since the Celrau who took you weren't privy to the particulars of the deal, we couldn't get the end-game out of them. We know more, now. A human friend was kidnapped by the Celrau and taken to the Hell Realm. Nathan went to hell to bring her back, and we learned a lot during her abduction and rescue."

"I need you to look at me, and not look away while I explain this next part," said Abbott. His voice soothed me, and I knew I shouldn't feel so comfortable, knowing he was a vampire, but he seemed safe. "The things I did when I altered your memories also shielded you, so no one would realize you're still a virgin from the energy of your aura. I applaud you for beginning the process of altering the symbols on your chest, but you're still marked. When I remove all pieces of myself from your head, you'll lose the shielding I put into your aura and brainwaves. It's imperative you don't remain a virgin, little one."

I started to speak, but he held his hand up to silence me. "I can see the trauma you felt when you tried to have sex. I can put a suggestion into your head, so you'll feel comfortable with the act next time, but Zeke was insistent I get your permission before doing so."

Zeke tensed beside me, but I didn't look at him. I stayed focused on Abbott. "Zeke was right. Enough has been done to my head without my consent. I'd really rather you just get rid of whatever you did, so I can have my memories back. I trust Zeke. I won't freak out on him." I was mortified at having to admit to everyone in the room I intended to lose my virginity to Zeke, but it just kind of came out.

No one made a big deal of it, though. It was as if they already knew. And, with Abbott in my head, he likely did. I resisted the urge to hide my face in my hands, but then realized maybe I was squeezing Zeke's hand too hard, so I let up a little.

"Very well," said Abbott. "I can hold you while I do it, or you can opt to let someone else hold you. I don't recommend you try to take this in without emotional support from someone, though."

I looked at Zeke, hoping he'd offer to hold me. The next thing I knew, I was in his lap, cradled in his arms.

"I have you, Teeny. Always."

I closed my eyes and rested my head on his chest, but then tensed as I heard Abbott inside my head. *I'll walk you through this as I release them to you. You don't have to speak aloud. I can hear your thoughts. If you want Zeke to know what you're saying, it's okay if you speak. Or, I can bring him in with us, so he can see and hear what's happening in your head.*

I considered his offer, but shook my head and thought, *No. Thoughts are supposed to be private. I don't think I want him in my head.*

*Okay. I didn't alter your memories of most of the abduction. I just removed the portion that would've told you they weren't human.*

Abbott gave my memories back to me a little at a time, and talked me through them as we came to them. Somehow, he made it so I was seeing them as if on a movie screen, instead of experiencing it all over again. It helped, but it was still hard. I'd never been naked in front of anyone before that night. Not since I was in diapers, anyway. My mom never even let the doctor see me in any form of undress. These vampires stripped me down to nothing, and looked at me *there* to make sure I was still intact in all ways. Apparently, you can be a virgin and not have a hymen, and they had to make sure it was still blocking the way. They hadn't raped me, but they'd pawed my breasts and handled my private parts. They'd sliced through my skin with their horrid claws, burned marks into my thighs, and coated themselves in my blood. I hadn't remembered them burning my thighs, but it made sense. The scars were different. More pronounced.

And through it all, Abbott reminded me this had happened over a year ago, and I was safe in Zeke's lap, and he told me how strong I am.

And I was right about Kirsten — my therapist had helped rescue me, and had moved us out of the way during the worst of the fighting.

*I hadn't rescued myself.* I'd known it, deep down, and I was relieved to finally not have the dichotomy of what I remembered versus what I knew to be true.

When we finally reached the end, I was a sweaty, sobbing mess. Aaron and Nathan had left, I guess to give us some privacy. It took me a few minutes to reorient myself, and it suddenly felt wrong for Abbott to be across the room. He'd walked me through something so painful, so embarrassing, so unbearably, *devastatingly* humiliating. And yet, he'd done it in the kindest way possible.

He gave me a gentle smile. "I can sit with you if I won't scare you. I believe Nathan and Aaron have made you a peanut butter and jam sandwich, which your mind tells me is your comfort food."

"Your powers terrify me, but you've earned my trust," I told him, and then what he'd said about my favorite comfort food sunk in. "You told them about the peanut butter and jam thing?"

He nodded. "You're in luck, because Aaron's wife happens to like organic grape jam, made without any extra sugar."

# Chapter Seven

*Zeke*

I scented every emotion Destiny went through as she got her memories back. I didn't have to see or hear anything to know what she was going through, and it broke my heart. Abbott can be cruel, but he can also be gentle, and her scent told me he was doing what he could to soften the impact of the memories.

By the time Nathan drove us home, Destiny was so far beyond exhausted I wished she'd give up and go to sleep. I wouldn't have minded carrying her inside, but she seemed set on remaining upright and speaking.

Her parents thought she was out of town for the weekend, staying with a friend who's attending UT in Knoxville.

Abbott had hinted at the fact she's in danger now because she's once again broadcasting her virgin status to those who can pick up on such things. Abbott tells me it isn't just that she's physically still a virgin, but she's also never had an orgasm. As far as he can tell, there's been no insertion of anything other than a tampon, and only that a few times because her parents forbid her from using them. She hadn't been allowed to swim when she was on her period.

Until she lost her virginity, she'd have to be protected by a strong supernatural capable of fighting off Celrau *and* demonkind. I'd told him if she was ready for sex this weekend I'd do it, but I wouldn't push for it. I hated having to do it on a timetable, and I was only considering it because I'd originally looked at this general time frame before I'd known about the urgency.

Nothing would happen tonight, though. She was exhausted.

When I walked her to the guest bedroom, I smelled fear.

"Nothing will hurt you in my home, Teeny."

She nodded, but her fear didn't abate, and I pulled her into my arms.

"There's a sofa in your room. Do you think I can sleep on it?" she asked.

I kissed the top of her head. "You can sleep in my bed, Teeny. Nothing will happen, but I need you to know you're safe."

I'd pushed her away last year because she was seventeen, and I've kept from so much as kissing her over the past month because I wanted the two of us to form a relationship apart from the one where I'd taken care of her last year. We've gone hiking, we've rollerbladed on the Riverwalk, we went to a trampoline park, and we've just sat on a cliff overlooking the city and talked. We've joked while eating lunch, and we've talked on the phone until the early morning hours. We're no longer victim and protector. We're friends who are attracted to each other, but who knows where things might go?

Also, I'd really wanted her to get her memories back before we started a relationship. I'd known what happened to her when she didn't. It hadn't felt right.

Now, however, she knew it all. The only barrier left was whether she could be comfortable with me if we took things to the next level. I had no doubt she could handle intimacy because I've held her in my arms enough to know she has no qualms about being close to me. She's an expert cuddler.

Sex is a different kind of intimacy, and I worried about how I should approach it. What could I do to help put her at ease? I'd run a million scenarios through my head, but in the end I'd just have to play it by ear.

She'd brought clothes and I knew she'd have pajamas, but my lion wanted her to smell like us. I gave her one of my shirts as I asked, "Can you wear this tonight, please?"

She nodded without saying anything, and went into my master bathroom and closed the door.

I stripped down to my boxer briefs, but then changed my mind and took them off to put loose boxers on. I usually sleep nude, so boxers would be more comfortable.

I turned the lights off and got under the covers to wait for her.

I frowned when I heard the shower turn on. I'd told her nothing was going to happen — had she not believed me?

I got out of bed and went to the bathroom. She hadn't locked the door, and I let myself in. The shower is towards the back of the room, and I stayed by the door to give her privacy.

"You don't have to shower before bed, Teeny. We're just sleeping tonight. You're exhausted."

"But you can smell better than a human, and I got all sweaty when I was crying."

I couldn't help but smile as I said, "Okay. I'll be in bed when you finish. We're just sleeping tonight. No stress."

\* \* \* \*

*Destiny*

He hadn't been joking about just sleeping. He'd held me through the night, but he hadn't tried anything at all. He hadn't even *kissed* me yet. Not a real one. He'd kissed the top of my head, and my forehead. Once he'd kissed the tip of my nose and my stomach had done backflips. I couldn't imagine what an actual kiss might do to me.

Still, having his arm over me, caressing me as I drifted off to sleep, made all the difference. Now that I remembered the Celrau in detail, I was *terrified* of them.

Sometime during the night he'd turned the bathroom light on and left the door open a tiny bit. He'd also put a bottle of water on my nightstand. The clock on his side of the bed told me it wasn't even five in the morning yet, but I needed to pee something fierce.

He has a wall of frosted glass in his bathroom to let light in while preserving privacy. No one can see in or out, but with the bathroom light on, they'd be able to see me moving around. Granted, they'd have to be on the roof, but I figured that'd be a piece of cake for a vampire. If a bad vampire was out there, he could bust through the glass and get me before Zeke even woke up.

I'd worked myself into a state of panic so intense I couldn't move to get up from the toilet when I heard Zeke's deep, soothing voice. "I'm outside the bathroom, Teeny. I can come in if you need me to."

Just like that, I was okay. He'd known I was afraid and woke up. Vampires weren't going to get me in his house.

"Thanks, but knowing you're close helps. I don't know what's wrong with me."

"Why don't you leave your underwear off when you come back to bed? My shirt comes past your knees, you'll be covered."

I froze as I considered the request. Did he want to finally fool around this morning? I eyed my backpack beside the sink and was glad it was in here so I could brush my teeth.

He pulled me into his arms when I opened the door. "You're safe in this house, Destiny. You're safe when you're with me. I won't let anyone hurt you." He walked us back to bed, but I was awkward as I got in.

He didn't say anything about me brushing my teeth, he didn't ask if I'd taken my panties off, he just situated me on my back, him on his side, and a shudder travelled through my body as he leaned in and kissed me.

I remember thinking he didn't have morning breath even though he hadn't brushed his teeth, but as soon as the thought skittered through my mind, all thoughts were history as I experienced my first *real* kiss. I've been kissed before, but never like this. His warm, strong lips teased mine until I kissed him back, like an erotic little dance, but with our lips instead of our feet and legs. Heat travelled through every nerve-ending in my body when he finally kissed my mouth open. I didn't know what to do with my tongue as his entered, but I couldn't breathe, either, because it felt like all the blood in my body went between my legs — except for a little that went to my nipples.

My hand rose and touched the side of his head before I realized it, but it felt right so I pulled him closer, even though he was already about as close as he could be.

His hand moved down my side and paused at my ribcage. I gasped when his thumb moved back and forth over my nipple, and my heart stuttered as he intensified the kiss. His tongue in my mouth made me want other parts of his body in other parts of my body, and my hips moved of their own volition.

I was a little embarrassed at the way my body was reacting, but he made a noise somewhere between a groan and a growl, and I realized he liked the way I moved.

His hand moved lower, and lower. Slow. So slow. Finally, his hand slid off the shirt and touched my knee. It paused a brief second, and my back arched as his hand moved back up the side of my leg, pushing the shirt up so his large, warm hand kept contact with my skin. As he got to my thigh, his hand moved on top of it, and when he went higher, it was between my legs.

I gasped, wanting him to keep going, and yet my body went tense, but I didn't shrink away.

His breath tickled my cheek as he kissed it and then put his mouth to my ear. "Baby steps, Teeny. Let's play around a little this morning. No sex yet — not until you're ready, but I have so much I can show you before we decide how far we should go."

"You wouldn't have known I got anxious all of a sudden if you couldn't smell it. Can we maybe ignore me being nervous?"

"No. This has to be good for both of us, and if I know you're uptight I'll do what I can to fix it." His hand touched between my legs and he pushed the lips together, over the little flap of skin they call a clit on the porn I've watched.

My breath caught as I realized *why* this little area's such a big deal. I moaned without meaning to, and my legs opened wider to give him better access. I've been taught all my life that only my husband can see me naked, and only my husband can touch my private places. I'd been horrified when the vampires had touched me, because they were taking that right away from my future husband. I thought they were sullying me.

Now, I didn't care about any of that. Zeke cared about me, and I was pretty sure I'd been in love with him since he'd held my hand in the emergency room and refused to leave my side.

My eyes flew open and my pulse raced even faster when he slid a finger inside me, and as our eyes met it once again felt as if I fell into his gaze. My mouth opened in a silent O, and his blue eyes held me as his finger moved inside me. Several strokes, and he touched a place in me that made my entire body go slack, and I made a deep noise way down in my chest I hadn't known I was capable of making.

I don't know how long his finger moved over the spot before my world went wonky. Maybe a minute, maybe five minutes. Time ceased to exist as he kissed me again while his finger stroked me from the inside until finally I was making all kinds of high and low-pitched noises because so much sensation was happening in my entire body, I couldn't contain all the feelings. I know some people have described it as fireworks, and I can understand why, but it wasn't fireworks for me. It was more like an atomic bomb, or a meteor landing in the ocean and moving the Earth, or something messing with the space-time continuum. It was so much bigger than fireworks, and when it was over and I tried to catch my breath, Zeke held my gaze as he lifted his finger to his lips and put it inside as if my taste was the best thing he'd ever had in his mouth.

If he'd done anything else, I think I'd have been embarrassed, or shy — but his brash enjoyment of me on his finger somehow made everything easier.

When I could finally speak again, I told him, "You look terribly smug, but I can't fault you for it. I had no idea it'd be like that."

I'd seen people orgasming on the porn I'd watched, but my new theory was that they'd had a pretend orgasm because I'm pretty sure they didn't experience anything close to what I'd just felt.

He kissed my forehead again but didn't say anything, and I asked, "Aren't I supposed to do something for you, now?"

"We aren't keeping score, and it'll be normal for me to give you lots of orgasms to my one or two. If you want to see me, or touch me, I don't have a problem with it, but only when you're ready."

"Will you help me?" I took a breath and admitted, "I've watched some porn online. I think I know a little about what to do, but I've never seen one in real life."

"Have you ever played with yourself?"

My face flamed hot and he gave me a gentle smile. "I masturbated all the time as a teen. There's nothing to be ashamed of."

"I could never get myself... it didn't work. I found all my parts, and, and..." I took a breath, closed my eyes to hide from his gaze, but then determined I'd look him in the eyes and answer his question even if I died of embarrassment. "I touched... everything, but it never made me... my hips never wanted to move like they did when *you* touched me."

The cocky smile was back, and I rolled my eyes but asked, "Will you show me what you like?"

He stood beside the bed and pulled his boxers down, and I inhaled as I saw how big he was. No way was *that* going to fit. He'd used a single finger in me and it'd felt big.

"Please don't be afraid of me, Teeny. I'll make it good for you, but that's later. Right now you're just going to explore me." He crawled back into bed, on top of the sheets and blanket with his penis touching the angles and planes of his abdominal muscles.

He put my hand on his thigh and slid it up until it was beside his beautiful — but much too large — penis.

"Be gentle with the balls and the head, but you can touch anywhere you want."

I hesitantly lifted my hand and poked it near the base, and he chuckled. "It won't bite you, Destiny. Here." He wrapped his hand around mine, and put our hands over the top of his penis and curled my fingers around it. "Think about simulating the sex act. So, we'll hold it like this, and then move our hands up and down."

He let go of my hand and reached into his nightstand drawer.

"Why do you have coconut oil in here?" I asked when I saw the jar.

"It works better if my cock is slick."

My face flamed hot again and he said, "Cock. It's a cock. You have a pussy and a clit. When you're ready to take your shirt off, your nipples are gonna be in my mouth — but no pressure. I can wait 'til you're ready."

My entire body felt as if it were blushing when he finished talking, and he chuckled again. "I adore you, Teeny. Let's get my cock and your hand slick."

\* \* \* \*

*Zeke*

It took every bit of willpower, in every cell of my body, to lie still while Destiny wrapped her tiny little hands around my cock and explored every inch of it.

I wasn't going to bring up a blow job, but she kissed the tip and put the head in her mouth, and my cock went impossibly hard. I froze, lest I freak her out by pressing into her mouth. She gave a few more licks before exploring me with her hands again, which was probably for the best. It would've killed me to lie still if she'd decided to explore me with her tongue.

God, but I wanted to be inside her. I had to wait, though. Had to take it slowly. I knew Nathan wanted me to make it happen today or tomorrow, and I would if she was ready, but if she wasn't then we'd just have to figure out how to keep her safe until... *fuck*. It really needed to happen this weekend. Aaron had sent someone earlier in the week to ward my house so no one could open a portal to Hell, but no way could we ward every place on campus she'd be.

But I would *not* rush this. If she was ready this weekend, great. If she wasn't, we'd have to find a plan B.

I let her play until I sensed she wasn't sure what else to do and was no longer as into it as she'd been, and I gently sat up. "As great as your hands feel on me, and the few seconds you had your lips on me were heavenly, but I'm not sure I can stay still much longer. If you want to watch me beat myself off, you can sit or stand beside me. If not, I can jump in the shower and take care of it."

I sensed her uncertainty, so I kissed her forehead and told her, "I'll jump in the shower in the hall bathroom, and you can get ready in here. I'll make eggs, steak, and bacon for breakfast. I have some canned biscuits we can bake, too." I wanted her to remain easily accessible, but it was a gamble to ask for it. I looked at her a few seconds before making up my mind. "I'll leave you another shirt to wear. Would you do me a favor, and wear it with no underwear? I'll throw on some loose shorts, with no shirt and no underwear. We'll both be covered, but... baby steps?"

I relaxed as the spicy-sweet scent of her arousal hit my senses, and smiled as she nodded and said, "Yeah, but it needs to be as long as this one."

# Chapter Eight

*Destiny*

"I told you I tried drinking and didn't like it."

"This isn't party drinking. It's a glass of wine with dinner. Have I led you wrong yet?"

He hadn't, and I shook my head but crossed my arms.

"You're so cute you're adorable, and you don't have to drink it if you don't want to, but I'm going to pour you a half a glass with dinner."

He'd marinated buffalo steaks that morning, and they'd soaked all day. This evening, he'd made country-fried pork chops and gravy while I worked on the mashed potatoes and made a broccoli casserole with tons of cheese. Now, he was turning the steaks on the grill, and I was wondering why we needed both buffalo and pig but figured it might be a lion thing so I hadn't asked.

Ten minutes later I realized he saw the pork chops, gravy, and mashed potatoes all-together as one side dish, with the broccoli casserole as another side dish, and the buffalo steaks the entrée.

"There's no way I can eat this much."

"Then you'll have leftovers to eat later."

I took a sip of my water as I watched him take a drink of his wine, and I rolled my eyes at him as I lifted the elegant wineglass and brought it to my lips.

The first impression wasn't great, but as the cool liquid slid down my tongue and I swallowed, I closed my eyes to savor the taste. And then I opened them as I felt warmth in my stomach. I took another sip, and the warmth in my belly seemed to blossom out to the rest of my body.

"Wow."

"Mmmm. I think a half a glass may be all you need, but I'm glad you like it."

"What, you insist I try it and then limit me?"

"Just tonight. I have no idea what'll happen between us later, but I want you sober for it."

"I thought you were getting me drunk to take advantage of me," I teased.

He reached for my wine glass and pulled it out of my reach. "Never, Destiny. I will *never* take advantage of you."

I was immediately sorry for my words. "That came out wrong. I was teasing — I know you won't. You've proven yourself too many times for me to have said that. I'm sorry."

His eyes closed a brief second before opening, and he met my gaze. "Thanks for that. I need you to trust me. It's important."

"I do. I wouldn't be here if I didn't." I shook my head. "Families who homeschool are closer than the ones who don't. I love my family, I'm close to my mom, and yet we lost some of it after I was kidnapped, and..." Kirsten had made me feel better about saying I was stripped naked and then cut with a knife as they carved symbols all over my body, but I still stopped before finishing my sentence. Zeke knew what'd happened without my having to tell him again. "I think I grew up in ways I wasn't supposed to that night. Or, maybe I should've grown up years ago and my parents kept me from the ways of the world. I'm glad they shielded me as long as they did, but now..." I sighed, unsure of how to word what I wanted to say. "I'm ready to grow up, but not with just anyone. I'm *so* glad you were in the woods this year for Halloween, and I think it would've been okay if we'd kissed and... *stuff*, before now, but I understand why you wanted us to spend time getting to know each other first."

He put my wine glass back in front of my plate, and sat back and looked at me a second. "I never imagined I'd fall for a human, much less one so tiny, but I think I fell for you last year. You'd gone through so much, but you were *so* strong. Maybe it's the homeschooling, but I've never met someone as young as you with such a sense of who they are."

"Why not a human? Do you think we aren't as good as you? Some kind of racist or... species-ist thinking?"

"No, but the rules about who can know about us are pretty strict, and I never wanted to be in a relationship with someone I couldn't be honest with." He took a bite, swallowed, and added, "Also, I'll have to be extra-careful with you. Humans break so easily, and you can't just *change* and heal if I get rough with you. It'll be okay, though. My lion wants to protect you and keep you safe. I don't worry about us hurting you by accident. He won't let me."

When I was younger, I believed everything my parents told me about God and Jesus as if it were absolute truth. As I've grown older and branched out in my studies, I'm no longer so sure. It isn't that my faith is shaken, it's that I'm not as judgmental as my parents. I knew in my heart I wasn't evil last year, and yet my parents were terrified I'd been tainted by evil. Their reaction altered my entire world view and made me think perhaps everyone — and everything — they proclaimed as evil might not be.

So now, I told Zeke, "My parents would likely be convinced you're evil if they knew about you, and listening to you talk as if there are two beings in your body has given me pause a few times." He started to speak, but I held my hand up. "Let me finish, please. I need to say this. You took care of me last year, and then this year you went out of your way to not take advantage of me, even when I practically begged you to." I don't want to be one of those people who constantly quotes Bible verses, but it felt right in this instance. Still, I didn't quote the whole thing, just the pertinent parts. "Matthew tells us Jesus said, 'Every healthy tree bears good fruit, but the diseased tree bears bad fruit … Every tree that does not bear good fruit is cut down and thrown into the fire.'" I shrugged, embarrassed to have quoted it, now that I'd said it. "You do good. Even as an attorney, you use your lion's senses to decide who you should defend and who you shouldn't. You have a moral code and you mean to do good. You aren't evil. Neither is Nathan, or Aaron, or even Abbott the vampire."

He caressed my cheek, and his finger pushed a stray bit of hair away from my face. "You've had a lot of stuff hit you at once. I think you're doing a fantastic job of dealing with it."

I shook my head. "After all the dreams about half-humans and half-beasts, knowing they were real was almost a relief. It meant I wasn't crazy, and the fact they saved me from the true monsters is a testament to the fact they… *you*, aren't evil."

"My sister doesn't know I'm a lion. She knows I was abducted and held prisoner, but we don't talk about it. She and her kids are coming to swim tomorrow. Her oldest daughter is your age, and I don't know if she'll be here or not, but the younger ones will."

"Isn't it too cold to swim?"

"The pool's heated. I turned it up a few days ago so it'll be warm enough for them. I generally keep it around eighty degrees if it'll just be me swimming, but I crank it up for humans."

"Should I leave before they arrive?"

"No. I'm hoping you'll stay and meet them. Swim with us. Have dinner with us."

"You want me to meet your family?"

"I do."

"I didn't bring a bathing suit," I hedged.

He gave me a mischievous grin. "I have a privacy fence. Nothing says we have to wear a bathing suit tonight, when it's just us."

The doctors and nurses had to see me naked in the hospital, but only little pieces at a time, and no one had seen me undressed since. I hadn't gone swimming over the summer because there'd been no way to hide my thighs, chest, or feet. Still, the thought of swimming outside — naked — in the dark with Zeke wasn't entirely bad, and I looked down as my face went hot again.

He chuckled. "I bought you a bathing suit a few days ago, just in case. It's a two piece, and those are easier to guess at since I only needed to get the how-big-around part, and not the how-tall part, too.

"I've never worn a two piece."

"Well then, it's about time you did. If you won't be comfortable in it tomorrow then we'll run out and get you something else in the morning, but I hope you'll be good with it tonight."

"A bunch of people saw my wounds at the hospital, but the football player's the only person who's seen them since they turned into scars." And he hadn't seen them all.

"You know I see *you*, right? I appreciate the fact you're beautiful, but it's who you are on the inside I'm attracted to. I look forward to seeing the beginnings of the tattoo on your chest, and I've seen a little of your forehead when I brushed your bangs aside to kiss it. Your scars don't define you, but they're part of who you are. If I care about you, I care about *all* of you."

I took another drink of wine and decided he'd had his finger inside me that morning, and I'd been in his shirt and no underwear all day. I'd survive a two-piece bathing suit.

"Yeah, okay. I mean, I want to see it before I agree to anything, but I'm not saying no."

And maybe if I was in a bathing suit, he'd do *things* to me again. We'd kissed a lot today, and he'd held me, and kissed my neck, but nothing else. There'd been *lots* of touching. He'd taught me self-defense stuff after breakfast, we'd watched Netflix a while, and then we'd cooked together. He'd had his hands on me at every opportunity, and he encouraged me to touch him and hug him whenever I wanted, too.

And I *liked* touching him. Not just because he has this incredible rock-hard body, but because it means he's allowed me to. It's like I'm one of the special people, someone he wants around, someone who has the right to walk up and touch him for no reason without asking.

The best part? His smile when I do. It's like he's happy I'm paying attention to him.

"Can I ask why you have such a goofy grin? Is it because I bought you a bathing suit?"

His question brought me back to the present moment, and while I wasn't sure I could completely explain it, I wanted him to know it wasn't just the bathing suit. "I've enjoyed my day with you. I like this."

His eyes softened and his smile went crooked. "I've loved our day, too. It killed me to walk away from you last year, but you were underage and you needed to pull your life back together with your family."

"I get it, but I'm glad circumstances brought us back together, and I'm *really* glad I had my dad's flashlight so I could see your lion."

We finished our dinner, though most of mine went into the refrigerator to eat later. The bathing suit looked like it would be thin shorts on the bottom and a decent amount of coverage on top, but the shorts were *so* short it felt like half my bottom hung out.

I stared at myself in the mirror. Bizarre symbols burned into my thighs, a single large complex image carved into my stomach, and dozens of small almost hieroglyphic figures on my chest. The tattoo would eventually make them into a collage of musical notes and symbols, but for now it was stark black ink and grotesque, hideous scars.

My head tilted forward and I looked at my feet. I'd worn long shorts and cropped pants most of the summer, with sporty sneakers to cover the scars on the tops of my feet. My ankles were white against my tanned shins, and I once again wished I'd been *anywhere* but the grocery store last Halloween. The van had been parked beside my car, and they'd pulled me inside and driven away without anyone seeing them take me.

I took a breath and came out of the bathroom. Zeke had a super-tall brick fence around his pool and it'd just be the two of us. He was going to see my scars eventually, it was better it happen now with a bathing suit on, instead of later when I might be naked.

He didn't ignore the scars, as I'd figured he would. Instead, he put his large, warm palm over the one on my stomach. "I can't imagine how bad it must've hurt. For me, seeing it reminds me of how strong you are." He traced part of the tattoo on my chest. "This, too. You're taking control, no matter how much it'll hurt. It's your body, and you'll decide how it looks."

I had no words, so I hugged him, and he hugged me back.

I dove straight into the water off the diving board, figuring if it was cold this was the only way I'd be able to get in. He'd been right about the water temperature, though, and I'd forgotten how much fun it is to swim when the water is warmer than the air.

I've often wondered what would've happened if I'd taken my phone outside and answered when my dad called. I hated lying to my parents, but there was no way I could explain why I needed to spend the weekend with Zeke. I'd talked to them that morning and made stuff up about the sightseeing my friend and I were doing in Knoxville, and how we might drive to the mountains and hike later.

When my dad couldn't get me on my phone, he logged onto our cellphone provider's website to see where I was, and saw the signal in town.

Thank goodness Zeke and I weren't having sex when he showed up, though with Zeke's hearing and sense of smell, he'd have probably known when my dad arrived, no matter what we were doing.

He heard him pull into the driveway, and he went through the house to see who it was. By the time I put jeans and a shirt on and made it to the front room, my dad was inside with his gun pointed at Zeke.

"Dad!"

"Get your things and let's go, Destiny Faith."

Until my abduction, I hadn't told my parents 'no' about anything since I left toddlerhood. I've carefully picked my battles over the past year, but I knew there was no way I could back down to him on this.

"I'm sorry I lied, but I'm not doing anything wrong. I know you won't see it that way, but I'm staying, and I'll see you and mom tomorrow evening."

My dad looked from me to Zeke, and I could see by the look in his eyes he planned to pull the trigger. It was as if I heard scripture in his head — *the man who lies with her shall die.*

My parents and their friends are prepared for the apocalypse. Or, better stated, the time period before the rapture, when they'll have to hold strong against the government and society for a few years until we're all *carried away*. They've trained, and they have armories set up with enough ammo to defend us for years.

However, my dad is human and Zeke isn't. Zeke moved fast, but not as fast as he could've. I guess he knows what he can explain as human, versus what would seem inhumanly fast. Nevertheless, in the blink of an eye he had my dad's gun out of his hand, and my dad on the floor, face down.

"I don't want to hurt you, Sir. I love your daughter and we're trying to figure some things out. I understand you want to protect her, but you can't walk into my home and draw down on me."

No one said anything for several long moments, and Zeke stepped away, popped the magazine out of my dad's Smith & Wesson M&P forty-five, ejected the round in the chamber, and set the unloaded weapon on a table behind him.

My dad stood slowly, his eyes on Zeke as he asked me, "What do you know about him, Destiny? I thought he was an attorney, but he's had serious training."

"He worked his way through college and law school as a bodyguard. He's had lots of training in how to disarm the bad guys so he can protect his clients."

My dad glanced at me, looked back to Zeke, and finally looked to me again. "You need to find a place to live, Destiny Faith. I'm not sure I know who you are anymore, and I can't let your actions influence your sibling's choices. It's bad enough you haven't gone to church in a year, but I've been following the preacher's advice to give you time and let you come back on your own." He shook his head and turned to the door. "If you want your things, you can get them after four o'clock tomorrow. If you haven't gotten them by Monday morning, we'll give it all to charity."

I was speechless, but Zeke spoke for me. "I'm sorry this is your decision, Sir. I'll have a truck there tomorrow to get her things. I hope you and your family will keep communication open with your daughter. Destiny needs her family."

He walked to him and offered his gun back, but not his magazine or the bullets.

"No, Zeke," I warned. "He'll have another mag on him. We'll have to get his gun back to him later, when he's calmed down."

My dad gave me an angry look as he spun on his heel and went out the door.

"I knew he had more ammo on him, and figured it was another loaded magazine," Zeke told me when my dad had pulled out of the driveway. "I wanted to see if he'd draw on me again, or take it and leave, but it's good to know you were looking out for me."

The air went out of me as I realized I'd further alienated my dad when I didn't have to. I moved to the kitchen to sit. I'd mostly dried off, but my wet hair was in a ponytail and I didn't want to get his good furniture wet.

"I'll have to take on more private lessons if I have a hope of affording an apartment, but I guess it's time. You once offered I could stay with you until I could find a place, is the offer still open?"

"You can stay here indefinitely." He sighed, cursed under his breath, and walked to me to take me into his arms. "I need to make a few phone calls. I'll take some friends from Drake Security with us tomorrow, and I'll arrange for someone from the Sheriff's Department to wait at the street and make sure everyone behaves."

I shook my head. "Bringing the police will make him mad, but I don't blame you. There's no guarantee he won't be loaded for bear when we show up tomorrow." I sighed, again, and stepped out of his arms. "I'll get your mop and take care of the water you dripped on your hardwood floors, then I'd like to get back into my bathing suit and swim some more."

Zeke stared at his feet a good five seconds before looking up. "Your dad has really bad timing."

Somehow, I knew he'd just altered whatever plans he'd had for the night, and it ticked me off. "Don't you *dare* change your mind about whatever was gonna happen tonight. I'm still the same person, making the same decisions. I promise I won't do something I wasn't already planning to do, but I need you to *promise* me you won't back off because of this!"

He shook his head. "I'm going out on the deck to make a few phone calls while you get the water off the floor. We'll talk about the rest of our night when I finish."

I opened my mouth to argue, but he shook his head again. "I need a few minutes, Destiny. Let me handle the logistics first, and then we'll talk. I promise."

# Chapter Nine

*Zeke*

It took me fifteen minutes to make arrangements for everyone to meet just off the interstate on the way to Destiny's house the next day so we could pull in as a united front. I also called my sister and told her something had come up and we'd have to reschedule.

Aaron promised he'd have an officer there for us, to be sure everyone minded their manners.

And now I was worried Destiny might have sex with me to ensure she'd have a place to live, but thank goodness my lion made me see some sense. She'd wanted me for weeks and I'd put her off. Also, she'd made a promise not to do anything she wasn't already planning to do, and I smelled truth when she said it.

If she was so distraught she wasn't emotionally okay for it, I'd know. Right? *Yes.* I'd know.

Before I went back into the house, I'd made up my mind to play it by ear — and smell — and see how the evening went.

She was sitting at my kitchen table, staring at her phone when I came in.

"Everything okay?'

"Yeah, I'll need to get my own cell plan tomorrow. They'll probably take me off theirs at the first opportunity."

"We'll do that in the morning before we get your things. You can give them your new number when you see them."

She nodded, and I told her, "We'll have a pickup truck and an SUV, and I can arrange for a box truck if you think they'll let you have your furniture."

"I don't know if they will or not, but it's only a few pieces and should fit in the back of a pickup. My guess is they'll have everything I can take out on the front lawn, so no one has to be invited inside."

"I'm sorry."

She shook her head. "Not your fault. I lied, these are the consequences. I hated lying to them — I knew it was wrong."

"They didn't give you a choice."

She shrugged. "I always had a choice. I took the easy way out. I owe them an apology, but they aren't ready to hear it yet."

She'd put her bathing suit back on while I was out back, and I still had mine on. "Come on, let's get something to drink and head back out to the pool."

When the lot beside my house had gone up on the auction block, I'd jumped on it, and then sprung for the fence and the pool. I may not be able to let my lion run as often as I like, but swimming laps in my human form comes a close second when I need to work something out. And right now, I needed to work the adrenaline out of my system. I can heal from most everything, but a close shot from a forty-five could be devastating and there were no guarantees I'd be able to make the *change* fast enough to survive the damage if I took a direct hit to the heart or brain.

I swam laps on my own for probably ten minutes. Destiny took up residence in a pool corner, out of my way, and I stayed aware so I could be sure she was safe. When I was finally exhausted and could think straight, I swam to her underwater and came up out of breath, pulling her to me as I gasped for air.

"Sometimes — now that I know you're a big cat — I can see the feline attitude."

I chuckled as I kissed the top of her head. "You aren't the first to call me an asshole cat. It's okay."

"I didn't call you a bad word!"

"No, but I understood what you were saying." I smiled, hoping she'd see I wasn't upset. "I wasn't born to it, but apparently because of the way I had to be taught control, my cat is more a part of my attitude than most who're bitten."

"I'm sorry my dad pulled a gun on you. Could he have killed you if he'd shot? I know you said you can *change* and heal, but is there a way to kill you?"

"I can be killed, but it isn't easy." Even for those who know about us, we aren't supposed to tell them our weaknesses.

"Does your lion like the water? Can he swim?"

"My lion *loves* the pool. He can swim, but he prefers to lounge in it, which is why I have the shallow area around the corner." It's an L-shaped pool, with the small leg of it between one and three feet deep.

"You built the privacy fence for him?"

I nodded. "Lions don't need to *change* on the full moon like the mythologies say werewolves do, but I need to let him out a good bit." I looked at the den I'd made for him in the corner of the lot, and then back to Destiny. "If I don't have to be anywhere early the next day, I often sleep out here as my lion. Not many shifters live in downtown residences, but with this lot, it's worked okay for me so far."

We swam, floated, talked, cuddled, and kissed for perhaps an hour. Sex doesn't work so well in a pool, so I didn't even try, but it was good to spend more time in each other's arms.

\* \* \* \*

*Destiny*

By the time we'd gone in and dried off, which took some time with a hair dryer on my part, I'd given up on him trying anything with me again. He'd left another of his shirts out for me, and I loved wearing his clothes. It seemed so *intimate*.

Still, I was surprised when I climbed into bed and he rolled so one of his legs were over both of mine, and his kiss took my breath away.

He kissed me until I was mad with desire, and he lifted his face to practically growl, "Don't wanna hurt you, but I need to make you mine."

"*Please* Zeke. I don't care if it hurts. *I need you.*" I sealed my mouth to keep from saying *please* again.

"You need to know a couple of things. I've never had sex with a human. I've told you some of the reasons, but it's also because my lion eyes come out when I'm…" he closed his eyes a brief second and I thought I saw a flash of pain. They were fine again when he opened them, but it made me remember how he'd become a lion. "If you see them, it's okay. It's still me. I'm in control, he just isn't far below the surface during sex." He sighed. "It's kind of important you do what I tell you though. Especially when he's near the surface. I won't hurt you, but I may have to walk away to get control if I think you're challenging us. Me." He shook his head. "Pronouns are hard, sometimes."

I think some women would've run away — or decided to find someone else — at the prospect of a lion peering in during sex. However, the look in his eyes when he told me… it was as if he was opening up and telling me a secret, and I knew in my heart it was important for me to accept *all* of him. Lion and human — both needed my love, respect, and acceptance.

"I trust you, Zeke. You won't hurt me. If you tell me to do something and I don't think I can, I'll explain. I won't just say no."

His mouth crashed down on mine, and my heart stuttered as the leg draped over mine pressed between them, parting my thighs so he could rest between my legs. He'd put boxers on, and he leaned into me so I felt his hard length on my bare private parts, but there was still fabric between while he kissed me crazy.

I grabbed at him as he moved down and kissed my neck, but he put my hands near my head and held them there as he kissed down my front, over the top of my shirt. *His* shirt.

My hands were freed as he moved to my crotch and lifted the shirt. I protested at first, when he put his *mouth* down there… until I felt the first long, decadent lick and pure desire swept through me, and then all I could do was groan and beg for more.

I knew what an orgasm was now, and I also knew he was getting me close and then backing off, over and over. I was nearly crazy with lust when he finally lifted his body over mine. He must've taken his shorts off when I wasn't paying attention, because it was all him now, with nothing between us.

My eyes flew open and I said, "Condom! I don't want to get pregnant!"

"Ssshhh. I'm wearing one. We aren't ready for a baby. I told you — I'll take care of you."

"When did you—"

He put a finger over my mouth and grinned. "I'm good, Teeny. Enough questions or I'll have to go down on you some more to get you all horny again."

His words alone were enough to remind me how much I wanted this, how close he'd had me to the edge, and how close I still was. My hips wiggled as he pressed the tip to my most private part, and then my eyes flew open again as he began to spread me open with his penis. *His cock*, I reminded myself. He wanted me to call it a *cock*.

"I'll go slow at first, unless you want me to go fast and get it over with."

I shook my head. "Slow is good. It's… *pressure*, but I thought it would hurt."

My head swam as he pulled out a little, pushed back in. "You're so tight, my little Teeny girl. I barely have the head in."

"You left my shirt on." It was hard to put words together with him inside me, but I'd expected him to strip me naked.

"Whatever it takes to make you comfortable." It looked like he was having to concentrate to string words together, too. I closed my eyes and rubbed my hands down his arms. His muscles seemed more pronounced, and I opened my eyes again to look. His arms were even more corded than normal, and somehow I knew he was having to force himself to go slow.

"It isn't hurting, Zeke. I'm good. I need more. I *want* more."

He pulled out and pushed in with more force this time, his gaze locked on mine.

His finger had been smaller, but he'd been able to find a magical spot inside me with it, and in some ways I think I'd enjoyed it more.

But this was... it was him spreading me open, claiming me, and he got pleasure this way, too. It wasn't all one-sided, and I desperately wanted to know what it would feel like with him completely inside me. I didn't care if it hurt, I just needed him *in* me.

"Please," I heard myself moan as he once again pulled out. "I want you. I want *all* of you."

"And you'll get me as I think you can handle me." He entered me again, the same speed as before, and I pushed my hips up to try to meet him partway.

His smile told me he liked me moving with him, and I braced my feet better.

Finally, he found a steady rhythm and I relaxed into it. I knew he wasn't all the way in, and I knew he was taking his time getting me used to him, but I was okay with it once he picked up speed.

Until he pushed harder, and went in farther, and my entire body froze as a high-pitched squeak came out of my mouth.

We both froze a second, and then his mouth was on my forehead and my temple as he apologized, but I said, "Don't you dare apologize. It just caught me off guard." I took his cheeks in my hands, looked him in the eye, and said, "I need you to give me everything. *Please* Zeke. I know it'll hurt, but can we get it over with?"

\* \* \* \*

*Zeke*

I'm so long, I can rarely fit all of me into a woman in the missionary position, and Teeny is *so* fucking short, I didn't think my length would all fit.

I should've been able to get a few more inches in her, but I didn't want to hurt her.

My lion, on the other hand, was on board with her plan. He wanted to get the first part over with so we could fuck like animals. Nathan had assured me the spikes on my penis would stay inside while I was with a human, and I had no reason not to believe him. Still, I worried a little.

The top of my bed's footboard has leather padding, exactly the right height for me to fuck someone bent over it. I wanted to see into her eyes, though, so it wasn't the ideal spot for now.

I slid off the bed and pulled her to the edge, so her ass was hanging off about an inch, and I showed her how to hold her legs up and out of the way. I spread my legs until my cock was the right height, and I entered her and pushed up. She was still soaked from all the teasing earlier, so it didn't take me long to find her g-spot with the head of my cock. She was even tighter from this angle, but her scent — and the expression on her face — told me any pain she felt was extra spice on the rest of it, so I pressed harder, and harder, though I kept my pace slow.

I hit bottom once and got a squeal out of her, and backed off enough to keep from doing it again. She felt so damned good around me, so fucking *tight.* My heart melted a little when she pushed her elbows in front of her legs to hold them in place so she could touch me and caress me.

I knew I was probably being too cautious. Nathan had talked to me about how careful I'd have to be with a human, but he'd also said they were a lot tougher than I thought. She was begging for more — I just needed to be sure she was enjoying it as I gave it to her.

I increased my speed and groaned at the way she accepted me into her. A few more scrapes over her g-spot, and her inner walls were gripping and moving with pleasure. I stayed in the same spot until she was ready to come, and then changed angles *just* enough to give her a different sensation. I instinctively knew she'd be able to take more of me at this angle, and I pressed farther, and farther, and then realized I was all the way in. I smelled pain and pleasure, but it was all sweet, nothing bitter, so I didn't back off. Some women like it when you bottom out inside them, and it looked like Destiny was going to be my dream woman in every way imaginable.

I paused inside her long enough to lean down and give her a kiss that threatened to break me. I knew she'd be able to see my lion's eyes, but she welcomed the two of us with her lips, her tongue. As I straightened, I touched her hand where it rested on my arm. "Rub and squeeze if it's good. Slap my arm if it's too much." I took a breath and tried to explain better. "My lion doesn't process words quite the same as me. We'll both know what it means if you slap my arm though."

She nodded, and I closed my eyes as I pulled out and pressed in.

* * * *

*Destiny*

I was glad he'd warned me about seeing his lion's eyes, but I wondered if he knew his voice changed too.

I wasn't afraid though. The lion hadn't hurt me in the woods and he wouldn't hurt me here.

At that moment, however, my brain wasn't capable of stringing those thoughts together, because Zeke's cock was doing the most *wonderful* things inside me. I couldn't move my hips to help with the speed from this angle, but I'm pretty sure I wouldn't have been able to control my lower body, no matter what.

In and out, in and out, and the stretch was on the verge of too much, and yet I *needed* to feel all of him, needed to be filled so completely, nothing else existed. When the front of his body touched mine — so I knew he was all the way inside me — I squeezed as tightly as my fingers could grasp his large, corded arms, and I vaguely remember screaming *yes* every time he filled me.

When my orgasm had hit before, it was like a tidal pool, where the waves get higher and higher until they eventually surge over the top and spill over, wave after wave after wave.

This one came on more like a freight train, barreling down the tunnel until it shot out the end and I was so overwhelmed with bliss, I couldn't breathe, couldn't move, couldn't *think*. My body moved and spasmed, and pleasure shot through my veins and saturated every cell of my body.

Zeke went faster, almost out of control, and then froze as he made a noise somewhere between a roar and a growl, and I felt heat inside me. Once he was still, I could feel my own muscles moving over his hard length, and my orgasm intensified as I realized we were both coming together. Our gazes met and I saw the man's crystal blue eyes, then the lion's all in amber and gold, then the man's again, and I squeezed his arms tighter, my fingers pressing into hard muscle as I pulled him to me.

Instead of laying across me when we finished, he reached behind my back and lifted me, his arms around me holding me to his chest as I grasped around his neck with my arms, and around his torso with my legs, and held on tight. I never wanted to let go, and he must've felt the same because he stood there a long time before he walked me to his bathroom.

He had me put one foot on the side of the tub, and told me to hang onto him for balance as he reached down to remove himself and the condom at the same time. He tossed the condom, and then his arms were back around me.

He'd turned one of the bedrooms of the old house into a bathroom, and the tub was custom made of tiles. I've seen smaller wading pools. I figured it would take forever to fill, but when he turned the knob the bathroom reverberated with the noise of four faucets filling the bathtub.

He shrugged as I looked at him in question. "I widened some of the doorways, and made other modifications for my lion too. Before I bought the lot next door and put the pool in, I needed to spend time inside as my lion. He likes lounging in the water, so I made a tub big enough for him."

"Why are we taking a bath?"

He stood me inside the tub and turned toward the sink. He pulled two gallons of apple cider vinegar out, as well as a small tub of Epsom salts. "I want to keep you from being sore later, if I can."

# Chapter Ten

*Zeke*

My little Destiny woke me with her mouth on me the next morning, and I talked her through the basics of a blowjob. She wasn't ready to take me to completion with it, but I went down on her when she reached her limit, and then let her help me give myself a handjob.

She wanted sex, but I wanted to give her twenty-four hours before we went at it again.

We went to the cellphone place to get her put on my plan, and then met Aaron and Nathan at Denny's in Cleveland before we headed across Highway Sixty into the middle of nowhere to get her things from her parents' house.

We were all outfitted with a GoPro unit on a live feed, and the officer at the road had a tablet supplied by Nathan, with video and audio from my unit, and video from everyone else's. I'm an attorney — I like to cover myself legally.

Destiny hadn't even tried to keep her old number, since the owner of the account has to okay its transfer. She'd thankfully been able to keep her phone, and had only needed a new SIM card for it. She called her dad from her new number when we were a few minutes away.

"We're almost there, dad." She waited for him to respond, and when he didn't, she said, "We have a pickup and an SUV, in case you let me take my bed. I love you, and I know you're disappointed in me, and I'm sorry. No one will threaten you, but you have to know they'll all be armed after you pulled a gun on Zeke." She looked at me as she took a breath and continued. "A police car will stay at the road. Zeke's boss wanted to make sure both sides use their manners. He called in a favor, so it isn't official and no one's writing a police report about it unless there's a problem."

My lion's hearing let me hear her dad say, "Everything from your side of the room except the furniture is on a tarp in the front yard. I figured you'd be in your heathen's bed. Do you *need* your bed?"

"Zeke's offered to let me stay in his guest room until I can find an apartment and get moved, but... Daddy, do we *have* to do this? I'll be in his guest bed for now, but it would be nice if I have a bed when I get an apartment." She sighed. "I understand I've made choices you don't approve of, and I'm sorry we have a difference of opinion, but I still love and respect you. I was wrong for lying, and I'm sorry for that too."

"You need to tell this to your mama."

"If you'll let her come outside and talk to me, I will."

My heart broke for her, but I could only act as her support system for this. My lion wanted to eat anyone who hurt her, but that didn't work when it was her family doing the hurting.

Her mother and father were outside when we arrived, as well as a line of six men behind them — every man open carrying, but their weapons were holstered, thank goodness.

I handed her father a clear plastic bag with his Smith & Wesson I'd kept the evening before, along with his magazine and the hollow point bullets I'd pulled from the mag and chamber. He accepted it all with a nod, and I began organizing how we'd load everything. We'd brought boxes and bubble wrap, and Destiny boxed the knickknacks as I put her clothes into the back of the SUV. Aaron put books and non-breakables into boxes and moved them to the truck, and Nathan helped Destiny with the bubble wrap.

Nathan told her to go talk to her parents, and he took over boxing the fragile stuff while I kept an ear out for what was said.

"I'm sorry, Mom. I understand why the two of you feel I shouldn't live here anymore, but I hope I'll still be invited to Sunday dinner. If you'll come, I'd like to invite you all to dinner once I get settled somewhere."

"Your car's yours," her mom told her, "and you're paid up on our insurance for another couple of months but then you'll have to get your own."

Her dad turned to the line of men and asked two of them to bring out her mattress, box springs, bed, and the table beside her bed. They turned and went into the house, and Destiny threw her arms around her dad when he turned back to her.

"Didn't think you'd need it," he told her, his voice gruff. "If this keeps you out of his bed, you can have it."

I accepted the large pieces from the men, wrapped the wood items in a blanket, and put them into the truck. I was careful not to do more than a strong man could do without help, but I showed off my strength. Her dad obviously respected muscle and power, so I showed him a little of what I had.

When everything was loaded, I nodded to her mom as I said, "Thank you, ma'am," and I looked towards her father and offered my hand as I said, "And thank you, sir."

Her dad looked at my hand a few seconds before he shook it. "I'm not handing her over to you. You don't have my blessing."

"I understand, Sir. I care about your daughter, and that means I want to see her have a good relationship with her family."

"Where's your family?" her mom asked.

"My parents were killed during my abduction when I was a child. My sister and her kids are all the family I have. I was held captive a long time before I was rescued. I'm glad Destiny managed to get away without having to spend months or years in captivity."

I smelled grief from her mom, and she said, "May God have mercy on your soul."

I knew the woman meant well, so I nodded to her again. "Thank you, ma'am. It was a long time ago, and I'm good now."

Destiny held onto her emotions until we were a few miles away, and then the waterworks started. Nathan was taking the truck to my storage unit and putting her bed and mattress in it, and then bringing the rest to my house. We'd go through it all, decide what stayed and what went into storage, and handle it over the next couple of days. She planned to start looking for an apartment, but I was hoping to convince her to live with me.

First, though, I needed to hold her while she cried. I found a pull-off and waved for Nathan to keep going as I stopped and wrapped my arms around my tiny little Destiny. I didn't know what to say, so I didn't say anything. I just held her, and offered her a napkin from my glove compartment when I thought she might need to blow her nose.

# Chapter Eleven

*Destiny*

Leaving my parents' house, knowing they were kicking me out and I couldn't come back, was harder than I thought it would be. I didn't want to talk about it, didn't want to deal with it, but my emotions got the better of me.

Zeke didn't ask a bunch of stupid questions, though. He just held me and let me cry.

As the oldest child, I think I learned more about how to take care of myself and others than my siblings. My dad took me hunting, taught me to change the oil and other fluids in the vehicles, and how to do basic maintenance on our four-wheelers and farm equipment. He never treated me like a weak little girl who couldn't handle getting dirty. When I wasn't strong enough to do something, he showed me how to work my muscles to make them stronger. We rarely had to take the time to exercise because we all chipped in with the garden, with reloading shotgun shells and bullets, and with all the other household chores as well.

But it was all done with love. My mom may have put our curriculum together and been in charge of making sure we learned everything we were supposed to — and then some — but my dad didn't leave it all up to her. He was aware of what we were learning, and when most kids are dissecting earthworms, he had me help him field dress a deer. He nearly always talked about what we'd learned at dinner with us. He made what we were learning relevant to our lives, whether it was history, math, or science. I'm pretty sure other kids didn't get to make a bomb when they were learning chemistry, or experiment around with various reloading weights and how to turn the firing results into scientific equations showing action and reaction.

And my mom found ways to help us gain confidence with what we'd learned. Instead of reviewing old material before she built on it, she gave me the textbook and told me to review it myself so I could teach it to one of my younger siblings. You can't half-way learn something if you're going to teach it.

My parents also worked hard to find our talents and help us hone them. My talent is music. One of my brothers is a math genius. My baby sister is already doing back handsprings and she's only four.

Some may say we were never allowed to be children, but I'd say we were never allowed to be brainless brats. We were allowed to play, but only after our work was done. I have many fond memories of catching fireflies, of swimming in the creek, and even making mud pies.

This wasn't a case of being kicked out when I hated my family and wanted to leave. It's true I wanted to move out and have more time to figure out who I am when not defined by them, but not like this.

* * * *

Zeke and I were unpacking the truck when Nathan arrived. The larger man got the keys to Zeke's car and told him he was taking me out to eat.

"Hold up just a bit," Zeke told him. "Let's move everything into the garage and then we can all go. I don't mind unloading everything, but Destiny needs—"

"It isn't open for discussion, Zeke. I'll take care of her, but Destiny and I are going to share a meal together."

Zeke looked to the ground a second, then looked to me. "He'll take care of you. If you don't want to go, you should tell him, but if you go, he'll make sure you're safe."

I looked back and forth between them, then looked to Nathan. "I get that you're the leader of the Pride and you can tell him what to do, but this seems a little rude."

"You can't talk to him like that," said Zeke.

Nathan held his hand up to silence Zeke, and told me, "You're human and I don't expect you to understand, but you need to respect our relationship. I took you under my wing the night we rescued you, and I may have handed the day-to-day responsibility over to Zeke, but the buck still stops with me. I'd like to take you to dinner so we can talk about where you are and where you're going."

The two of them looked at each other, Nathan nodded, and Zeke came to me. I had my hair in a ponytail but a few strands had come loose and he tucked them behind my ear. "He won't force you to go if you don't want to, but you should go."

"You have to do what he says," I told him. "Even if he were planning to rape and torture me, you'd have to tell me to go with him."

"I've seen people who are forced to live under a bad leader. It's true they have to do that kind of thing, but you can tell they aren't happy and don't want to. You've heard how Nathan saved me, and I've told you how much I respect him." He kissed my forehead. "Draw your own conclusions, Teeny. Listen to your gut."

\* \* \* \*

As Nathan pulled up to a restaurant in a bad section of town, I looked around, wary.

"You're safer here than just about anywhere I could take you. It's a biker bar, and I'm friends with the club." He put the SUV in park and shrugged. "Once they know you're one of mine, they'll make sure you're safe if you ever need to go to them for help."

My heart skipped a beat. "I'm one of yours?"

He pulled the keys from the ignition and gave me a gentle smile. "Zeke's mine, you're his. That makes you one of mine." He shook his head. "When I sent him with you to the hospital, I did so because his sister's daughter's about your age and I knew he'd take good care of you. Also, he used to be human, and has more humanity than those of us born a lion." He sighed. "Zeke hasn't had a human girlfriend since he was bitten, so I assumed there was no danger of him seeing you as…"

He looked out the front window a moment before looking back to me. "I never expected him to view you romantically. If he'd acted on it last year, I'd have put a stop to it. However, enough time has passed I hope this is more than rescuer and rescuee." He took his seatbelt off and opened his door. "Let's go in and get something to eat. I'm getting ahead of myself."

A large man with his whole arm tattooed was behind the bar, and he nodded at Nathan and me as we walked in. Nathan directed me to the back, and a waitress moved a rope and showed us to a table on a raised platform. The inside was nicer than I expected – lots of beautiful stained wood, brass, and chrome.

"Their burgers are excellent, but you can't go wrong with anything on the menu."

"You're sure we're safe here?"

"I know you've been shielded from society all your life, but it's time you lived a little. Tattoos don't make someone evil, just like your brands and scars don't make you evil."

I froze at the realization he'd called some of them brands. I hadn't known the marks on my thighs were brands instead of scars until Abbott walked me through my memories. Did Zeke know, too? Should I tell him? Did it matter?

"I'm sorry," he said. "I didn't mean to cause you distress."

"It's okay. You just caught me off guard. I'm not used to seeing tattoos that are so… visible. I've never been in a place like this."

"Have you ever been on a motorcycle?"

I shook my head. "We have ATVs. Or, I guess *had*. My family has them, but I don't anymore."

"They're still your family. Give them time."

"You don't understand. I broke the rules. I'm an outcast now."

"For everyone's sake, I hope that isn't the case."

"They'd freak if they knew about you and Zeke."

"Which is one of the many reasons they'll never know."

We placed our order with the waitress, and Nathan told me, "Drake Security awards from six to ten college scholarships a year. We have seven active at the present time, which means we still have a few to give away." He pushed a business card to me. "Go online to the web address on the back of the card and fill out the application. If your GPA is above a three-point-two, you'll get a full ride scholarship, including books and dorm fees."

I eyed him a few seconds before saying, "My GPA will be a perfect four when the semester ends, but I have a feeling you already know that."

He nodded. "Guilty. My point is, if you don't want to

live with Zeke, you don't have to. You have options. I also believe, if you don't have to pay for school, you'll have enough to live on without having to add any students to your schedule."

My eyes teared up and I looked down. "Does Zeke know you're making this offer?"

"No, but he'll be on board with it. He doesn't want to trap you, Destiny. If you want to live with him then that's where we both want you, but if you don't, I can have you in a dorm within two weeks, and I can stick you in one of our local safehouses until we get you moved into student housing."

"I asked him if I could stay with him until I found an apartment, and he said I could stay indefinitely."

"You don't have to give me an answer on the dorm right now, but if you can fill out the online form today or tomorrow, it'll help us get everything taken care of in time for us to pay your tuition for the next semester."

"Why are you doing this for me?"

"I own part of Drake Security, but the scholarship fund is already allocated, so please don't look at this as me paying for your college. I'm just facilitating the paperwork for the company to give you the scholarship. As for the rest," he leaned back and grinned, "I told you, I took you on when we rescued you. We did what we could to keep you safe from the Celrau, and determined your family and their guns could protect you from anyone else who came after you once you were home. At the time, you didn't leave your property much, since you were homeschooled."

He shrugged. "You were better off with us backing out of the picture and letting your family take care of you, but now you need us again." He chuckled. "Stubborn-headed, *insane* human. What possessed you to go into the woods on Halloween, to the place you were abducted and tortured?"

"I hoped it would give me closure."

"Did it?"

"No. Abbott gave me that when he gave me my memories back."

"Yeah. Have you talked to a plastic surgeon about what it'll take to get rid of your scars?"

I shrugged. "More money than I imagine I'll have for a really long time. I've started a tattoo on my chest, but it'll take some time to finish it. I'm apparently a wimp, and can only take so much before I'm in tears."

"Nothing wimpy about that at all. If you talk to Kirsten about it, she'll probably tell you some of it's emotional crap, too, and not just about the physical pain."

Yeah, she'd mentioned it, and she was probably right, but I didn't want to talk to Nathan about it. "There's an organization that helps pay for plastic surgery for victims of violent crime, but I haven't had the nerve to apply for help. There's no guarantee they'll help, and I'll have to take pictures of all the places I want worked on before I can apply." I focused on the water droplets trailing down the outside of my glass of sweet tea. "The only pictures I've let anyone take are the ones the police took for evidence."

"I know a plastic surgeon who'll work with us on price. If you'd like, I can make an appointment for you to talk with him. I know it'll be a lot to get everything worked on at once, but it'll be the cheapest route. I won't offer to pay for it, but I'll finance it for you at no interest, and we'll work out a payment plan you're comfortable with."

I opened my mouth to object, but he shook his head and smiled. "You're one of mine. This means I'll help you to help yourself, and you won't argue with me about it."

I turned my palms over and looked at them. I'd sliced into them when I left the hospital, and altered the symbols they'd carved into me, so they looked like flowers. My left hand was a rose, my right hand was kinda-sorta a tulip, if you looked at it just right.

"I want to get my forehead done more than anything, but I'd also like to get my stomach and thighs done. I took control of my palms, and I'm taking control of my chest."

"And your feet?"

I blanched. "Yeah. I'd love to be able to wear sandals again."

A biker in a leather vest with patches all over it came up the steps, and Nathan motioned to him. "Duke! Come sit with us a second and meet Destiny?"

He talked to us for maybe ten minutes, and by the time he left I was feeling a little silly for having thought he was a bad guy.

I told Nathan, and he chuckled. "He can be a very bad guy when it's called for. If anyone lays a hand on his wife then there's a good chance he'll make them hurt in ways you can't imagine. But, he won't hurt someone without reason, and if he saw someone bothering you, he'd make them stop."

"Was he serious about Zeke and I coming to their party next weekend?"

"Yes, and it'd be good for the two of you to stop by during the day, when the kids are still around and it's a family atmosphere. The more of the RTMC you meet, the better."

A few more bikers stopped by and chatted, and by the time we left I no longer viewed the leather vest with all the patches on it as a scary, bad thing.

Viper — my tattoo guy — walked in as we were leaving, and I was surprised he was wearing one of the biker vests, too. He'd been recommended as someone who could cover scars with his designs, and I was *so* glad I'd found him. He talked me through how to breathe while he worked on me, and I'm not sure I could've gone through with it if someone had just tattooed me and expected me to deal with the pain. We talked a few moments, and he hugged me as we left. It felt good to know someone Nathan hadn't needed to introduce me to.

As Nathan pulled out of the parking lot, I asked, "You wanted me alone, without Zeke, so you could gauge whether I'm considering moving in with him because I want to, or feel I have to — right?"

He nodded and I said, "I appreciate it. I need to talk to him before I make a decision, but thanks for looking out for me."

* * * *

*Zeke*

I trust Nathan with my life, but I was still on edge while he was gone with Destiny. He's my liege and his word is law. If he told me I couldn't be around her, there was no higher authority to appeal to.

I walked onto my porch as Nathan pulled my car into the driveway, and stood waiting for him to get her out of the car and bring her to me. She carried a box with the food she hadn't eaten, and I smelled fries and a burger. Grass fed beef — had he taken her to the RTMC bar?

I smelled Duke and Bash on her as she came up the steps, but I didn't say anything about it as I opened the door to let them in.

"I need to put my food in the fridge," Destiny said, as she quickly made her way through the house toward the kitchen.

I looked to Nathan, hoping for answers, and the fist around my gut relaxed at his smile.

"Everything's fine, Zeke. Give me a hug and I'll go. Destiny can tell you about our conversation."

Everything is always right with the world when Nathan hugs me, and today was no different. He's larger than me, and way more powerful, but he also loves me. Most are terrified of him, and I have a *very* healthy respect for his power and the weight of his office — but I don't fear him.

I heard Destiny behind me as I closed the front door

after Nathan, and I turned to her with a smile.

"I'm glad the two of you have each other."

Her words caught me off guard. I could see why she'd be glad I have him — but I couldn't see it the other way.

"He's the King of the Lions, Teeny. He doesn't need me in his life."

"Yeah, I think he does. The two of you have a special connection, and no matter how powerful he might be, those connections are important. Never doubt the role you play in his life. I may not know much of anything about him, but I recognize the fact you've helped keep him grounded. You've helped him stay in touch with feelings I think he has trouble remembering."

It was true he'd personally worked with me when he'd found me. A man as busy as the Amakhosi wouldn't have been faulted for handing me off to others, but he'd kept me with him and taken charge of teaching me control.

"How did you get to be so smart?"

She shrugged, obviously uncomfortable. "My parents, my church, our work helping others less fortunate? I don't know. I can just see it."

I pulled her into my arms as she stepped near, and her body molded to mine like it belonged.

"What did you and His Majesty talk about?"

"He's going to arrange for me to get a college scholarship through Drake Security."

Once she'd explained the offer, I realized His Majesty had once again swooped in and saved the day. Of course, he'd also messed with my hopes of having Destiny live with me, but I couldn't argue with his logic. Having her choose to stay with me when she had options would mean so much more than having her stay with me because she didn't have much of a choice.

My first response was to tell her, "Nothing has to be decided today. We'll move your clothing and other basic necessities into my guest room. I hope you'll sleep in my bed, but I want you to have your own private space, too. Once you've reached some decisions, we can figure out our next steps."

Now, two hours later, she was in her room with the door closed, playing her violin.

My lion paced inside me, desperately wanting out, but I didn't dare *change* without warning her ahead of time she might encounter him. I instinctively knew she was playing a super-challenging piece as a way of shielding her emotions — something to focus on rather than the problems she apparently didn't want to have to face at the moment.

Her parents had hurt her, and she had so much uncertainty in her life. The closed door wasn't a rejection of me, it was just Destiny needing space.

I walked outside, stripped to nothing, and dove off the diving board. I could hear the violin as I swam laps, so I knew when she changed from fast to slow. When the tenor changed again, her violin literally pouring waves of grief into the air, I stopped swimming to listen more carefully.

A sniffle. And another. I leapt from the pool and stalked towards her window. A minute later there was no doubt she was crying as she played.

The man might have continued to give her space, but the lion wouldn't consider it. I shook the water from my hair as my body heated to dry the drops on my skin before I took a few seconds to slide into my jeans. I took long, fast strides into my house and through it.

She hadn't locked her door, and I didn't knock. She stopped playing when I walked in, and I gently moved the violin and bow to the side before I took her into my arms and held her. Tears streamed down her face and the scent in the room was full of grief. My Destiny was never going to cry in a room alone again — not when there was breath left in my body.

Her arms circled my neck, her face buried in my throat, and now huge, wracking sobs tore from her.

"I have you. You're safe, and we'll figure everything out. I *have* you."

"I'm a mess," she sobbed. "I'm so sorry."

I kissed the top of her head. "Today's been hard. No one would expect you to hold it together. Cry all you need to. Scream and yell and hit things if it'll help."

She stopped crying and looked at me like I was crazy. "Hit things?"

I kissed her forehead. "Yeah, it works for me – though *you* apparently play beautiful music instead of punching inanimate objects. I have ice cream in the freezer. If you have another comfort food preference, I'll go buy whatever you want."

# Chapter Twelve

Five months later

*Zeke*

I've never been so happy to move someone out of a dorm before in my life, but I had to admit her moving into it had been the right decision. I'd been disappointed, but I'd made sure to be supportive when Destiny had moved in.

She'd spent plenty of time at my house, and lots of weekend nights, but this had given us our space as we've gotten to know each other better.

Also, it went a long way toward healing her relationship with her parents.

Was I crazy for asking her to marry me so soon? I didn't think so, and Nathan was the only one with the balls to bring it up, but even he was in favor of it — once we talked.

She and I had an open invitation to Sunday dinner at her parents' house, and we both went, *every* Sunday. She'd found a non-denominational church in town she felt fit her needs, and her parents had gone with her to it once. They didn't exactly approve, but they didn't disapprove, so it seemed to be working out for all of them.

However, this Saturday, we'd be married in her parents' church by the pastor who'd been over her since she was a small child. It was important to her, so I was good with it.

My family went to church maybe four or five times a year when I was growing up. I was exposed to religion without it being pushed down my throat, but I hadn't been back inside a church since I'd been bitten and turned. Not because I turned my back on it, but because I'd only gone when my parents had taken me, and they were no longer around to take me.

Destiny and I'd had hours and hours of conversation about faith, religion, spirituality, and God. We tried to make it work with what we know of the supernatural world, but I couldn't get permission to tell her about the gods of old who still occasionally walk among us, so there were some things I couldn't tell her.

None of that really mattered, though. She uses her beliefs as a foundation for her morals, but not as a club to beat people over the head with.

And I love every inch of her, and wouldn't want her any other way.

Much to my surprise, Destiny's become good friends

with Tippy, a little deer-shifter mated with one of the RTMC wolves. Nix was out of town at a big biker thing, and Tippy had planned to stay home alone from the beginning because she doesn't do well in raucous crowds. My little Destiny planned to stay at Tippy's place for the two nights before the wedding, and then she'd live with me after the wedding — with her parents' blessing.

Or, as close to a blessing as I'm ever likely to get from her dad. I'm not sure he exactly likes me, but I think he's relieved to have her married off.

I lost my parents, though, and I know how important it is to have them around. Nathan's been like a father to me and I appreciate him more than I'll ever be able to tell him, but I still miss my mom and dad.

So, I'll do whatever I can to facilitate a good relationship between Destiny and her family. Even if it means biting my tongue around them a whole helluva lot.

* * * *

*Destiny*

I have one year of college under my belt, and I've yet to make my first B. Every grade has been an A, but I've had to work my ass off to make it happen.

One of my professors arranged for me to play my violin with a special practice session of the Atlanta Symphony a few weeks ago, and I've since been invited to audition for a seat. It's only a two-hour drive, and the opportunity to play with them is incredible. If I'm not selected, the experience has given me the courage to audition for the Chattanooga Symphony in the fall.

So many directions my life can go, but right now I'm focused on starting my life with Zeke. He had the bedroom on the other side of the bathroom turned into a closet for me, even though I don't have anywhere near enough clothes to fill it. He says I will, eventually, but I don't see it. Still, it was a nice gesture.

We've moved my things to his house over the past weeks. I didn't have that much, but it's nice to see my things mixed with his on the mantle in the living room. He's also taken more pictures of me than is reasonable, and has about a dozen of them around the house. I don't really mind though, because each picture reminds me of a fun day with him — rock climbing, or paddleboarding, or even the time I convinced him to take me to the beach for spring break and we went snorkeling.

There are people who say they never completely got over their first love, and people who say you need to date around to get an idea of what you want. I say, if you're never going to get over your first love, and he treats you good and the two of you are great together... what's the big deal about dating around?

I'm glad we've had time to date without living together. I think it was important for me to have my own place — even if it was just a dorm and not an apartment.

But now? I'm ready to spend the rest of my life with this man. He feeds my heart and soul, and he says I do the same for him. Zeke and his great big, beautiful white lion. I need them both in my life.

# Chapter Thirteen

*Destiny*

Zeke and I hadn't had sex for two weeks before the wedding. It wasn't really planned, but I was on my period, and then we were so busy with the final wedding plans, and he's been working long hours in preparation for being gone for our month-long honeymoon. When we finally started fooling around earlier in the week, I mentioned it might be good to hold off until our honeymoon, just to make it a little more special.

He'd given me a mock glare, but had smiled to let me know he'd indulge me.

So now we were walking up the sidewalk of a rented vacation home on a little island off the Maine coast. He said I'd liked the beach, he'd hated the heat, so this was where we were going. I got the smell of the ocean and the sound of the waves lapping the shore, and he got temperatures in the seventies.

None of that mattered though, because I'm not a virgin anymore and sex with Zeke has turned into one adventure after another.

Aaron flew us to Maine on his private jet, and Zeke had arranged for a boat to take us to the island. Still, even though we hadn't had to deal with commercial transportation, it'd been a long day when we finally arrived.

I know Zeke, though, and I wasn't about to let him pull the, "You're tired, let me help you get to sleep," thing. I may be human and fragile compared to a shifter, but I'm not a baby and this was my wedding night.

And it'd been sixteen days!

Much to my surprise, however, he brought our suitcases in, set them in the bedroom, and met me on the deck where I was listening to the surf crash on the rocks below. I could see a little of the waves as they turned white in the dark, but it was overcast and pretty dark.

Zeke surprised me by wrapping his arms around me from behind and saying, "You have entirely too many clothes on, *wife*."

I leaned back, into him, and said, "I don't have any underwear on under my skirt."

His vocal chords changed enough for me to hear a bit of a low roar as his chest rumbled behind me, and the next thing I knew, I was bent over the balcony, my long skirt over my back, the warmth of his hands at my hips, and his hard length entered me from behind.

This was the rough, coarse, wild man with a lion inside, and I loved it when he took me like this. I knew he'd make love to me later, and I'd enjoy that, too.

But this? The feral, raw, animal side of him? Spikes and slivers of ecstasy shot through my veins when he entered me with no preamble, no warning, no finesse. One minute we were standing, cuddled like an ordinary couple, and the next he was inside me, moving fast and hard as spasms of pleasure ripped screams from my throat.

Twice, I haven't wanted him to be rough with me, and both times he stopped before the head of his cock pressed inside. He knows by my smell whether I'm good with it or not. He's never going to do anything I don't want, and I love that he can get physical and demanding and know it's okay. My body and psyche were damaged the night he met me, but I was whole again — in large part because of the way he'd shown me how great sex can be with the right person.

And this was the perfect way to consummate our marriage. He loves having sex outdoors but it'd taken me a while to be okay with it. I mean, sure, there's a huge privacy fence around his pool, but what if someone *heard*?

He'd installed speakers and played movies with people running, or fighting, or doing other things to mask any orgasm noises I made, and then had made excellent use of the diving board.

I was hooked. There's nothing quite like looking into the night sky as you orgasm, and tonight, when he brought me to a screaming, pulsing, out-of-control release, I knew my noises were covered not only because no other houses were near, but also because of the sounds of the ocean crashing onto the rocks below us.

Tonight, he apparently was okay with me being tired, because as soon as the orgasm faded, he had me undressed and inside as he told me, "That was one. I'm going to make you orgasm nonstop until morning, and then *maybe* I'll let you take a nap."

I wrapped my arms and legs around him and accepted him inside me once again as I moaned in bliss. I knew he'd make it good, and I'd never mind anything this man wanted to do to me.

*The End*

Stay up to date on Candace's new releases by signing up for Candace's newsletter.
http://eepurl.com/W_Cij

**Keep reading for an excerpt from *The Dragon King*.**

If you enjoyed *Hallowed Destiny*, you may also like the other books set in the same universe, though in different series.

*Chattanooga Supernaturals* series, paranormal romance:
- The Dragon King *(Aaron Drake's story, and the first time we meet Duke and Brain)*
- Riding the Storm *(Kendra and Eric's story)*
- Acceptable Risk *(Bethany, Ranger, Mac, and Jonathan's story)*
- Careful What You Ask For (*Britches story*)
- Hallowed Destiny – Forged by Darkness
- Uncaged (*Ghost's mother's story*) Feb 10

*Only Human* series, urban fantasy
- Only Human
- An Unhuman Journey
- Unhuman Acts

*Rolling Thunder Motorcycle Club* Series
- Duke
- Brain
- Bash Volume I
- Bash Volume II
- Bash Volume III
- Horse
- Nix
- Gonzo (*where we first meet Britches/Briana*)
- Ghost

Dark Erotica Shorts from the world of The *Chattanooga Supernaturals*
- Pride (*A short story featuring The Lion King*)
- Indentured Freedom: Owned by the Vampire

The Safeword series, intense BDSM contemporary romance
- Safeword Rainbow
- Safeword: Davenport
- Safewords: Davenport and Chiffon
- Safeword: Quinacridone
- Safeword: Matte *(Sam and Ethan Levi's story, we first meet Frisco and Cassie)*
- Safeword: Matte – In Training
- No Safeword: Matte – The Honeymoon
- No Safeword: Matte – Happily Ever After
- Safeword: Arabesque *(Frisco, Cassie, Isaac, and Cam's story)*
- Safeword: Mayday (TBA)

Check out other books by Candace Blevins at candaceblevins.com.

Keep reading for an excerpt from **The Dragon King.**

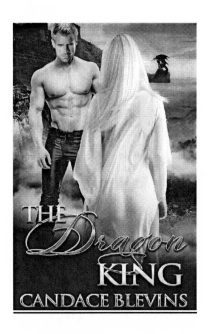

# The Dragon King

## by Candace Blevins

Book one of The Chattanooga Supernaturals, paranormal romance with claws...

Aaron Drake is nine thousand years old and one of the last remaining European were-dragons. With no female Dragons, his only hope of children lies in his grandmother's dying words. "The Swan Princesses may be the Dragons' only hope."

Sophia Siyanko is the first Swan Princess without at least one brother to take the throne in Aaron's long memory. However, her father chooses her husband when she's twelve, and sets the date for her twenty-fifth birthday. She is sequestered in her father's mansion, raised by governesses and tutors to be the future King's arm candy, and Aaron's options are limited.

But then Sophia escapes her father's compound a few weeks before her twenty-fifth birthday. Determined to escape or die trying, she comes to Aaron for help.

To protect her, he'll have to fight every swan and eagle on the planet, most of the wolves, and all of Faerie.

# Prologue

*Aaron*

Sophia is the most adorable two year old I've ever seen. Fluffy blonde hair, rosy chubby cheeks, and a laugh that makes my heart soar.

I turned to her father, the Swan King, and chose my words carefully. "Raul, you're sure this is the best course of action? I know you're still grieving over Angelique's death, but can you truly prepare Sophia for a life of leading your people if you keep her a prisoner in your home her entire life?"

I could only get away with asking this question because I'd helped raise and train Raul, helped prepare him to take the crown when he beat his brothers and won the throne.

"I did my best to protect my wife from supernaturals, and a damned *human* hunter took her out. Sophia won't leave the walls of the castle until she marries, and hopefully whoever wins her will follow my lead and also keep her behind protective walls. She won't see the same fate as Angelique." His voice was firm, didn't waver, and let me know further conversation on the matter would be met with hostility.

Sophia is the first Swan Princess without at least one brother since before I was born, and by my best guess I'm around nine thousand years old. Give or take a thousand.

Swan Princesses are usually given to other royalty as a way to unite families and sometimes species, but they never have a hope of the throne. Their brothers are required to fight each other for power, the strongest and most cunning winning the crown.

Instead of finding another wife to give him sons, Raul is arranging for a contest between the other swan royalty, with the strongest being allowed to care for her until she turns twenty five, and then marry her and eventually take the crown. Personally, I think Raul wants to step down and find a way to join his dead wife. The grief of her death still holds him.

I've trained the past seven Swan Kings, including Sophia's father, Raul. I know him well, and I know he loves his daughter. However, he still feels such pain over his wife's slaughter, and I worry about the decisions he's making.

There is precedence amongst some other supernatural species for keeping Sophia in seclusion, finding a suitable King, and not giving her a choice in who she'll marry. However, watching the toddler play and laugh and flirt, my heart hurts with the knowledge she'll grow up with no control of her major life choices. Or, likely the minor ones, either.

She's such a happy baby, so full of life and adventure. I hope her life turns out better than most fairy tales.

\* \* \* \*

Ten years later, my heart aches as the court Herald announces me into the Swan King's mansion for Sophia's final unchaperoned lesson. I've been coming to the mansion once a week for a four hour session since she was six, but this must stop once she becomes a teenager, which in swan lore makes her a woman.

I'll be allowed to come four times a year for an all-day review session, but will never again be alone with her.

After today she'll have a chaperone or minder with her anytime she's with a man besides her father — or husband, once she's married.

I'm going to miss my time with her. In my busy life, my half-days with the Swan Princess have been the sunshine of my week. Sophia is a special child — so smart, so willing to learn, and a joy to be around. My heart is happy when I'm with her, and we most often go to our spot near a manmade waterfall on their property so we can talk without worrying so much about being overheard. Someone from the house can see us, but our words are drowned out. Sometimes, though, my favorite part of the day is her smile when I arrive and she skips to me for a hug. Today will be the last time she'll be allowed to hug me for no reason, just because she's happy I've arrived. My heart hurts as I wrap my arms around her and tell her I'm happy to see her.

We walk to our spot, sit on our rock and I open a few books as I give her another to hold. The rushing waters may provide white noise to block our voices, but we still need to appear as if I'm teaching her.

"You know this is the last time we'll be alone, right, Soph?"

Sophia looks down, takes a breath, and raises her gaze back to mine. "I know. I'll miss my time with you."

"And I'll miss you, but you're a Princess and one day you'll be Queen, so this is the way it has to be. I'll be back to review the important stuff, but there are some things I've taught you that I won't be able to review with you out loud. I'll try to write it in a notebook and let you read it, so you'll remember, but there is some danger in that so I won't do it every time."

"Why take the risk? If I'll never rule, never make a difference, why put yourself in danger?"

"Because I'm grooming you for power, Princess. No one knows for sure what the future holds, and to fully do my job I can't just teach you the palatable parts of your history. I understand your father wishes to shield you and protect you, but I can see the strength in you."

Sophia sighed. "I'll still see you at social occasions? Not just the four times a year you're allowed to come for review?"

"Yes, and I may or may not be allowed a dance with you. I will certainly not be able to take you outside for a conversation."

She nodded, and I carefully said, "Sophia, if ever you find yourself in need of a protector, get a message to me. Your father and Cyrano will look after you, but if you find yourself without their protection I hope you'll feel comfortable letting me keep you safe."

Shaking her head, Sophia said, "Cyrano scares me. My latest governess tells me when I'm a woman I'll appreciate him for his strength and resolve, and I must remain meek and quiet around him while I'm a child."

I wanted to wring Cyrano's neck for frightening her, as well as the governess's for giving crap advice, but I had to walk a fine line. "I'm sorry he scares you, Princess. I would advise you to speak to your father about it, see if he can intercede on your behalf."

"You always do that."

I tilted my head and let my eyebrows rise, and Sophia explained. "When we're just talking, I'm Soph or Sophia, but when you're thinking politically, you call me Princess."

"Yes, because this is the way an elder speaks to someone of royalty. I'm your teacher, I know more than you, but I must also show respect. It's a balance, Sophia."

She shook her head. "I don't know what you are, and my father either doesn't know or won't tell me, but I'm positive you're royalty, too. I've learned to tell the difference between someone with their own power who addresses me and my father as an equal while using all the right words, and someone with no power who addresses us with the same words but a completely different energy."

I hoped my smile showed how pleased I was with her insight. "You make me proud, Sophia. I hope you'll keep your suppositions to yourself, though."

She nodded. "Of course, and I hope someday you'll trust me enough to tell me what and who you really are."

I needed to be sure she understood my offer, so I repeated it. "Do you understand what I'm saying, Soph? If you ever need help, a protector, a friend, an advisor…If you're ever in trouble I hope you'll find a way to get a message to me."

# Chapter One

*Sophia*

I'd been planning my escape for eleven years, and tonight I'd either fly to my freedom or die trying.

I was to be married to Cyrano on my twenty-fifth birthday, in seventeen days. However, I was determined it was never going to happen.

Tomorrow, my governess was meeting with people in Charleston on my behalf to assure the wedding would go off without a hitch. Since I was never allowed off my father's property, if someone couldn't come to me then I had to send my people to them, and the caterers had decided they couldn't make yet another trip to go over last minute details.

I knew they wouldn't, it was part of my plan.

I'd sent my governess away earlier this evening so she could stay in a hotel and be present for the seven o'clock meeting tomorrow morning, and then make surprise visits to check in with the florist and a few other vendors.

I'd brought books up from the library to my bedroom, asked for my tea service a little early, and told everyone I wasn't to be disturbed.

I'd been nervous and anxious for months, so no one paid any attention to my scent anymore. I was perpetually on edge.

It was eight fifteen, and I figured I'd have until the guard shift change at three in the morning before anyone realized I was gone. My current guard wasn't likely to decide he needed to put eyeballs on me, but I knew they'd look in on me at shift change. They always did.

Swan shifters need to *change* a minimum of four times a year, at both equinoxes and both solstices. However, since my father didn't want me leaving the property, when I *changed* they immediately turned me back human. I'd never been allowed to even *try* to fly. The rest of the time I wore an anklet my father had brought someone in to create especially for me — it kept me from turning into a swan any other time of year.

I'd spent years combing through the books in our extensive library, and was convinced I'd found a way to defeat the anklet. Years ago, I'd also learned from one of our servants that it was possible for a virgin to *change* without the normal flogging to rip enough skin away so we could shift into our swan form.

She said one could use a knife to cut a seam from one foot, up the outside of the body, from armpit to fingers on the bottom of the arm, and then fingers to shoulder on the top of the arm, over the head and scalp, skip the right arm and go down the body to the right foot, and then as the left foot comes out and forms, use the claws to rip a seam in the skin from the right arm so it can pull free.

I had a very sharp crafting knife and hoped it would do the job.

Meanwhile, I'd long ago figured out how to defeat the alarm system at my window so I could at least open it and get fresh air. I used a screwdriver to carefully remove the contact from the window's hardware, taped it to the stationary contact on the window frame, and then slowly opened the window, making sure everything stayed put.

Taking a breath, I poured the hot water from my tea service into the plastic bin that normally held items in the storage area of my closet.

It'd taken me years to assemble the herbs and roots without arousing anyone's curiosity, and I now dumped them into the bin and stepped into the scalding water. Trusting the concoction would do its job, I bent with the knife, stuck it into my foot just under my ankle bone, and began the excruciating task of literally skinning myself.

I'd known it would hurt, but this was worse than the traditional flogging a virgin must undergo in order to *change*. I was more than determined, though, so I did it fast and didn't make a sound, even though I wanted to scream and cry.

Halfway through the process I knew I'd been wrong about having hours until my escape was discovered. They were used to smelling fear on me, but not pain, and certainly not blood. I was going to have to fly for my life and hope they couldn't keep up. I cut faster, and my blood flowed into the hot water at my feet.

As the knife finally reached the outer edge of my right foot, I stood and imagined myself a swan, thought of how it felt to *change* after I was flogged, and breathed in relief as I felt the transformation happening. The herbal concoction worked, and the anklet would end up in the water once I turned into a swan and it could come off my foot. As I *changed*, it only took a few slices with my claw to rip the skin on top of my right arm enough for it to come free of the skin and turn into a wing, thank goodness.

I made it onto the window sill, looked out at the Waccamaw River, and knew if I couldn't figure out how to fly within a few minutes, and the crash landing didn't kill me, I needed to find an alligator and hope he was hungry. I was going to either escape or die — I couldn't live the rest of my life trapped in this house, and being forced to marry Cyrano was the final straw. People might make fun of the Princess trapped in the mansion with anything her heart desired at her fingertips, but *this* Princess preferred freedom to riches.

I jumped from the ledge, stretched my wings, and breathed in relief as the wind caught them and I soared instead of plummeting. I beat my unfamiliar wings, pointed my head the direction I wanted to go, and it just somehow *worked*.

I'd spent years on borrowed tablets from various servants, looking through Google Earth so I could find my way to Chattanooga, Tennessee, and the offices of Drake Security. I had no idea where Aaron Drake lived, but figured I could find him at work.

I followed the coast to Savannah, Georgia, fighting the ocean breeze, and figuring out how this brain parceled the information I'd taken in with my other brain. I managed to access what I needed to make the journey, and I followed the coast as I learned to soar, turn, dive, and climb. The winds coming in off the ocean were brutal at times, fluffing my feathers the wrong way until I lost control and only regained it by luck. I soon discovered I needed to get higher to keep from being buffeted by the sea breeze, but going too high made it hard to see landforms well enough to navigate when there weren't many lights.

I didn't know how much of a head start I had, so I kept moving even as I experimented, terrified they'd find me and haul me back to my father's house.

When I reached Savannah, I found what I was sure was the interstate and followed the line of lights north. I was exhausted when I reached what had to be Macon, and I continued north a little ways before making a right turn, hoping I could find the wildlife refuge and a relatively safe place to get some rest. I was so tired, and terribly uncomfortable in this body, but needed to stay a swan until I made it to Chattanooga. I wasn't sure I could cut myself open again, and besides, I no longer had the knife.

I only rested a short time in a tree top before I flew north, once again following the interstate. I was sure this wasn't how swans normally navigated but it was the best I could manage. I breathed a little easier as I went over Atlanta, knowing my journey was close to an end. I often swam miles a day in either the lap pool or the endless pool, but I'd never been so tired in my life.

When I made it to Chattanooga I headed towards the Tennessee River, followed it until I recognized their unique Aquarium building, and then followed the streets out of the downtown area to the old school building that housed the Drake Security offices. My landing was far from graceful, but I made it into the woods across the street, found a tree limb I hoped would be safe, and waited.

## ABOUT THE AUTHOR:

Candace Blevins lives with her husband of eighteen years and their two daughters. When not working or driving kids all over the place she can be found reading, writing, meditating, or swimming.

Candace writes BDSM Romance, Urban Fantasy, Paranormal Romance, and is currently writing a Motorcycle Club series.

Her Safeword Series gives us characters who happen to have some extreme kinks. Relationships can be difficult enough without throwing power exchange into the mix, and her books show characters who care enough about each other to fight to make the relationship work. Each book in the Safeword series highlights a couple with a different BDSM issue to resolve.

Her urban fantasy series, *Only Human*, gives us a world where weredragons, werewolves, werelions, three different species of vampires, as well as a variety of other mythological beings exist.

Candace's two paranormal romance series, *The Chattanooga Supernaturals* and *The Rolling Thunder Motorcycle Club*, are both sister series to the *Only Human* series, and give some secondary characters their happily ever after.

You can visit Candace on the web at candaceblevins.com and feel free to friend her on Facebook at facebook.com/candacesblevins and Goodreads at **goodreads.com/CandaceBlevins**. You can also join **facebook.com/groups/CandacesKinksters** to get sneak peeks into what she's writing now, images that inspire her, and the occasional juicy excerpt.

**Stay up to date on Candace's newest releases, and get exclusive excerpts by joining her mailing list!**

YOU'VE REACHED
"THE END!"

BUY THIS AND MORE TITLES AT
www.eXcessica.com

eXcessica's YAHOO GROUP
groups.yahoo.com/group/eXcessica/

Check us out for updates about eXcessica books!

WRITE A REVIEW!

*Readers, in the age of ebooks, remember that you are in control of separating the good from the bad, the wheat from the chaff.*

*Please take a moment to go back to the site where you purchased this book and leave your opinion, however lengthy or brief, about it.*

*You can also go to larger sites (Amazon, Barnes and Noble, GoodReads) and leave your reviews there as well, whether you made your purchase on their site or not.*

*Make your vote count! Your opinion will help other readers make their future purchasing decisions in regards to ebooks.*

5-17

DISCARD

CPSIA information can be obtained
at www.ICGtesting.com
Printed in the USA
LVOW12s1539100517
534023LV00001B/67/P